In the Heat of Texas

A Toombs Sullivan Adventure

Tom Pilgrim

In The Heat Of Texas
A Toombs Sullivan Adventure
Copyright © 2020 by Tom Pilgrim

In The Heat Of Texas is a work of fiction. The characters are creations of the author. However, extensive research was done into the history of Texas after the Civil War, especially concerning the Texas Rangers and the Comanche Indians. Much of the action is based on records of their encounters.

ISBN: 978-0-578-76739-0 (Print Edition)
ISBN: 978-0-578-76740-6 (E Book Edition)

Dedicated To
My Cowboy And Cowgirls

Bert

Sheri

Christie

Fiction By Tom Pilgrim

The Taste Of Paradise

In The Heat Of Texas

Non-fiction By Thomas A. Pilgrim

Faith For Today And Tomorrow

The Master Has Come

The Roads Jesus Traveled

Behold The Man

The Man From Galilee

They Came Together In Bethlehem

The Light of Bethlehem Shines On

1

He rode up a little hill and sat there on his horse for a moment looking out toward a town, one he was surprised to see. He had not at all expected that. He wondered how many people lived there. Surely there was a place to find something to eat. He took off his hat, wiped the sweat from his forehead, and tried to spit, but could not. There was nothing in his mouth but dust. He put his hat back on, nudged his horse forward, and rode slowly down the other side of the hill.

A few dusty minutes later he came into the town. A man was sitting on the porch of a small store, the first building he approached on the edge of the town. The man was leaning back in a chair with his feet propped up on a post.

He looked like he was half asleep, but roused up and spit out tobacco juice when he sensed that someone was near.

"Say, Mister, is this Texas?"

"Hot as the devil ain't it?"

"Yeah, it is."

"It's Texas."

"What's the name of this place?"

"Marshall."

"No, I said what's the name of this place?"

"Marshall!"

"No. I ain't no lawman. What is the name of this town?"

"This here's Marshall, Texas. What's yore name?"

"Name's Toombs Sullivan."

"Toombs? You mean like a place where you lay dead people and close them up?"

"No, like a grandson named after his grandfather."

"Where ya hail from?"

"Georgia."

"Figured you for a Reb from maybe Georgia or Alabama. They come through here all the time looking for Texas. How was it that you got here?"

"I saw a small wagon train a few days ago. I just followed their tracks. I guess there's been so many coming this way they made a road of sorts."

"Yep. They all come here, stay a day of two, load up supplies, and then they go on west of here, lookin' for it."

"Looking for what?"

"Texas."

"Is it always this hot?"

"No, Toombs Sullivan. Sometimes it's hotter than this."

"How do ya stand it?"

"If you can't stand the heat, ya don't belong in Texas."

2

He walked down the road from Chattanooga and through a village called Chickamauga. The ravages of war were seen everywhere. He had witnessed the destruction all the way from Virginia in his weeks long trek toward home and hearth and happiness, and maybe even health again. He had lost so much weight, but still hoped his wife would recognize him, if she was still there at their farm.

Long ago he had stopped getting any letters, even if she had written any they would never have caught up with him. He had written a few, but it had been some time, how much time he did not know.

The closer he got to the farm the better he felt. His spirits were lifted up. There was almost a feeling of joy surging through his body, but not much joy, just a little. And the surge was not a gushing, just a slow ebbing.

He passed by a farm house he remembered, but could not remember the name of the people there. It was some old man and his younger wife, though she was much older than Toombs was. He remembered that much about them. He saw her sweeping off the little front porch of their house. He waved at her, but when she waved back it was obvious she did not recognize him for it was not the wave of recognition, just a slight lifting of the hand and the awkward glance, not even a stare. But it was all right, no hurt feelings on his part.

He would never have any ill-will toward another human being as long as he lived. Enough of that. It was over and done, and now there was peace. That is what he was wanting now, even the peace that passes all understanding. The phrase jumped into his mind from somewhere back in his early years. Yes, it was a Bible phrase he remembered. He wanted a peace beyond understanding and comprehension and description. He had had enough of war and killing and suffering and hunger and cold and thirst and death. He wanted life now, the life he had before. And he was not far from it, just a few more miles. He made it this far, so he could make it that much further.

Soon he came around the last curve in the road and felt his heart beating faster. When he exited that curve, he then turned his face toward home. He saw it still standing down on his left and thought, thank God. Two large oak trees were in front of the house, not far from the road. The old barn was almost down, over half of it having fallen in, but the house was still intact it appeared. He took off his hat for a moment and pushed his long blond hair back away from his forehead. He felt his unshaven face, knew it was dirty, grimy, and he knew he smelled bad. His tattered clothes were hanging off him. His piercing blue eyes zeroed in on his house. He began running, forgetting about being weak and tired and sick and run down. He cut across the field and then across the yard. He stopped at the front steps, one of the three was missing. Half of the porch had fallen in, but the front door was still there. He walked up on the porch, stood in front of the door, touched it, and it slowly opened. When he stepped inside, he saw the house was almost empty with only a few pieces of furniture lying around on the floor. Pieces of the large mirror lay scattered across the living room. He propped his rifle against the chimney and pulled a pistol from his belt, laying it on the mantel. He walked back through the house to the kitchen and saw more of the same destruction with the stove turned over and the pipe lying down. He then went in the two bedrooms where the old mattresses had been sliced open, the bed frames broken, and a chair or two destroyed, another shattered mirror and some clothes were lying on the floors. At least enough of his clothes remained, though old, and he could at least have something fairly decent to wear. His wife's dresses were piled up, some of them being ripped and cut.

His wife Constance, where was she? And the boy, Little Toombs, where was he?

He began calling her name, "Constance! Constance!" And all the while wondering why he had not done that sooner.

He raced out the back door, still calling out to her, "Constance!"

There was no sign of anyone anywhere.

He walked around behind the barn and then he saw them, two graves with tree-limb crosses marking them. They had been there for some time and were almost grown over, but there was no mistaking what they were.

The shock of that was worse than anything he had felt during the war. Could it really be them? He drew closer and closer, and then threw himself to the ground on top of what must be her grave judging from the size of it.

He buried his face in the dirt and reached out his hands and scooped up two handfuls of the dirt. He began crying, sobbing, shaking, all the while calling out her name, "Constance!"

He lay there for a long time until there was a passing of the light and the coming of the shadows all around him.

He slowly pulled himself up, knowing there was no more crying to be done for he was all cried out and had completely run out of tears. Inside, he would go inside. Food, was there anything to eat? There were apples from the tree, still small now, but big enough to eat. At least they would be something. He quickly ate several small ones, the juice running out of the side of his mouth. He wiped it away with the sleeve of his right arm.

He went inside to what was left of the mattress he and Constance had shared for years. He lay down on it, and, being physically and emotionally drained, fell into the sleep of faraway lands and scenes and peaceful valleys and flowing rivers . . . .

And as he came near the home place, he saw her sweeping the front porch. She looked up and saw him, dropped the broom, and ran down the steps and across the yard toward him. He put down his rifle just as she came to him, and took her in his arms. As he held her his senses were filled up with all that was her. Then he saw his son come out the front door, and he knew what it was like to be finally home . . . .

When he woke up the next morning, he knew what he would do. It had come to him in the night, perhaps in a dream, perhaps in some waking moment, but his resolve was as firm as if he had thought it out and planned every detail.

He gathered all the clothing that was still usable, a knife he had left behind for his son to have, an old pair of boots far better than what he now wore, a hat his father had given him years before, and then he put the clothes in a bag that he could throw over his shoulder as he put the hat on his head and mashed with his foot the hat he had been wearing. He had changed his clothes, placing the rags in a pile, and then went to the corner of the room and removed a board from the floor. He reached in the hole and pulled out a jug he had placed there before the war. It contained their life savings. He had forgotten how much was in it, but it did not really matter. It was Yankee money, and Yankee money could get him some food down the road. He smashed the jug on the floor, picked up the money and stuffed it in his pocket. He slid the knife and scabbard inside his right boot. Then with determination he went outside, a man with a mission.

He went first to the barn. The old dried out boards and timbers readily caught fire. Then he went inside the house and built a small fire in such a way that it would quickly spread. He placed the pistol back in his belt. It was an Army Colt .36 caliber cap and ball revolver he took off a dead Yankee. Then he took the rifle, a .44 caliber sixteen shot lever action Henry repeating rifle he took off another dead Yankee, threw his bag over his shoulder, and walked out of the house to the road. He watched as the flames in the house started small, began to spread, and then began leaping through the rooms, coming out the windows and the door, and climbing up the walls to the roof.

Then he turned around and walked away. He went down the road toward LaFayette. Perhaps he could catch a ride to Atlanta. There was bound to be work there, enough work at which he could earn enough money to get him on the road, the road to a new life in for him a new place.

3

When Toombs Sullivan reached LaFayette he realized there was no ride to Atlanta, but he bought bread and cheese and gorged himself. He sat on a bench in the town square and talked with an older man about the war and what happened.

"I remember you, Sullivan. I heard about your family. I'm sorry. What you gonna do now?"

"I'm just leaving here."

"I know it was a hard thing being in the war, but not being in it was pretty hard as well. Both them armies came all around here trying to find each other. See the Presbyterian Church up there. It was used for a hospital. And also that big house up there on the right was used by the Yankees. They put their horses in there. If I'd been able, I would have killed all of em, but I weren't."

After eating Sullivan said goodbye to the old man and left. If he could get to Resaca maybe he could catch a train going to Atlanta. He knew that General Sherman had taken his army down to Atlanta from Chattanooga.

As he walked toward Resaca, he passed through what was called Snake Creek Gap between two mountains. Sherman had sent part of his army through there to try and cut off the Confederate army at Dalton. But they had already fled south, and there was a great battle at Resaca.

After Sherman had gotten to Atlanta, he kept the railroad repaired so his supply line from Chattanooga would remain open.

Toombs Sullivan was sure the trains were running now. If he could hop a train he would make it all right . . . .

She came to him in the place where the willow trees grew. The blossoms floated to the ground as she walked under the limbs, gently brushing them with her shoulder. The blossoms gathered on her shoulders and in her hair. Her skin was soft and sweet as she pressed her lips on his cheek. He held her in his arms and vowed he would never let her go, never let her go. He would hold onto her forever. He felt her breathe on his neck, and the gentle breeze blew her long hair across his face . . . .

He woke up the next morning as he arrived at the train yards in Atlanta where he saw a lot of work being done. In spite of what he had heard, all of Atlanta was not burned down, but a lot of it had been destroyed. Already efforts were being made to get it in order again.

He saw a man who looked like he was in charge of the rail yard work. He walked over to him and spoke.

"My name is Toombs Sullivan. I'm looking for work."

"I'm Roscoe Ennis. You up to what you see being done here?"

"Sure."

"Good. Ben! Put this man to work!"

Ben Wright walked over toward him and said, "This way."

He led Sullivan to where men were laying out ties and driving in spikes as they laid new rails.

"You gotta be really good at this to drive spikes in tandem with these other guys here. So being new you'll be bringing over the ties and layin'em down. You'll be told the exact spot, so don't worry about thinking. Just do what you're told. You look a little worn down. Can you do this?"

"Yep."

"Have at it."

Sullivan joined the others who were carrying the ties. It was hard work, the ties were heavy, and he was weak, but he was determined to do it. His future relied on this. He would be able to eat on a regular basis and would gain his strength back. And this kind of work would get him in shape for the journey he would make, a journey into tomorrow.

By the end of the day he had made a favorable impression on Roscoe Ennis and Ben Wright and also the men he worked with laying out the ties. One of them spoke with him when the day was over. He was a burley looking man, medium height and wide, dark beard, black eyes, and was still wearing the brown pants and checkered shirt he had been given in the war, but he had no cap on his head.

"So you're Toombs, what, Sullivan? Right?"

"Yep, that's it. And you."

"John W. Culpepper, but they call me Pep."

"Okay, Pep."

"You new here?"

"I am."

"Got a place to stay?"

"No, I don't."

"Me and Pistol over there got a room in a boarding house. There's a big bed and a small bed. You can room with us. I sleep in the big bed. You can sleep with me. Best part of it is the food.

All you can eat and it's really good. Best food I've had since before the war."

"Sounds good to me."

Pistol Pugh came walking over, grinning from ear to ear. He was a small man, small in height and small in weight. He must have been close to forty, Sullivan thought, as he stuck out his hand. He took off his Rebel cap and revealed a head with not much hair left, but what there was of it was long, stringy, and dark.

"Sullivan."

"Pistol."

With the work day over the three men walked along where the warehouses had been. Now there was nothing but the charred remains, burned timbers, twisted metal, and piles of ashes. They went about a mile and came to a street where there was a row of houses.

They went inside the third one on the left and were met by Sally Atkins who owned the house.

"Take a seat in the dining room, Boys," she said happily. Sally Atkins was a widow woman, her husband having died shortly after the war began. She had been able to survive by taking in borders. She was a large woman with a head full of silver hair pulled up on top and in back of her head.

"Miss Sally, this is Toombs Sullivan. If it's fine with you he'll be staying in our room. He works with us, so he can pay. Sit, sit down."

"Good. Always glad to have another. Here's the chicken. Rest'll be out shortly."

They passed the platter around and the six men at the table devoured the chicken as the beans and cornbread were brought out.

"Where ya from," Sally Atkins asked.

"Up the road a ways between LaFayette and Chattanooga."

11

"Hell of a fight up there," Pep said.

"Yeah, I know."

"Did ya have people there?"

"Nope. Folks died before the war. Just me."

"What about ya home place?"

"I sold it before I went to the war. Figured I'd get killed. Thought I would never come back there if I survived it. I did."

"Want a biscuit?"

"Thanks, Miss Sally."

"But you didn't want to go back there?"

"Nope. I don't want to dig in the dirt the rest of my life. Looking for something else, some place else."

"Got any place in mind?"

"Nope."

"Where ya from, Pep?"

"Dahlonega."

"How about you, Pistol?"

"Dahlonega."

"You boys gold miners?"

"There ain't no gold in them thar hills. That's why we are here."

"I see."

"You know, Sullivan, it's funny what a war will do to a country and a town like this and a man. It just has a way of disrupting everything. It'll turn a place upside down and a man as well. And nothing ain't never the same again. You don't feel the same. You don't want the same. You don't think the same. It's just different. Everything is different."

"You're right about that, Pep. Nothing is the same."

"Only you turned yourself upside down before the war."

"Yeah, I guess I did. But I'm gonna land right side up. I'm one of the unlucky ones who lived through it. Would have been better to have died and be remembered than to live and be forgotten. That's why I won't be here for long, just long enough to leave."

"You got a funny way of talkin'."

"Yeah. I laugh myself to sleep every night."

Sally Atkins had listened to the conversation between the men. There was something about this new one that made her wonder. She had always been the mothering kind, which is why she now took these drifters in and tried to give them a home. And it seemed to her this new Sullivan needed a home more than the rest. She saw in him a sadness and a loneliness that tugged at her heart. She wanted to ask him what was the real truth about his life, but dared not do it.

4

Nine months later the signs of Spring began appearing. The flowers and trees were blooming and the birds had come back. Geese could be seen flying over Atlanta, heading north again.

There was a lot of construction in the city, and with it a feeling of hope for the first time in a long time. But reconstruction was often cruel, and the hopes of many people were dashed as the new good life they had wished for was not appearing. The North had won the war, and the South was being made well aware of that fact.

During those months Sullivan had managed to put away some money. He had enough to buy a horse, outfit himself for a journey, purchase cartridges for his rifle and paper cartridges for his pistol. He still had his knife. He bought some more clothes. He was strong now, stronger than he had ever been, the work having been good for him. The color had come back to his face. He had gained some weight, and his face had filled back out. He was a healthy six feet tall and must have weighed about two hundred pounds.

One day after work he said to his two friends as they walked toward Miss Sally's boarding house, "Boys, I'm leaving."

They were both surprised, and Pep said, "Where ya goin'?"

"I'm going to Texas."

"Texas?"

"That's right."

"Why? When did you decide that?"

"The day I got home from the war. There was nothing there for me, and so I didn't even slow down. I just walked right on by the old home place. There was some little boy out in the front yard on a swing hanging from the limb of an oak tree somebody put up for him. I waved at him after he yelled out at me. He said, 'Where you headed?', and I said I was going on down the road."

"Why Texas?"

"A lot of people are going to Texas. It's a land of opportunity."

"It's a good place to get skinned alive by the savages or have yore pretty blond curls hanging on some Indian tent."

"I'll take my chances."

"That's a chance I would never take. I had enough of fightin' and all that."

"Me too," chimed in Pistol.

"I did too. But I got nothin' here, so why not just give it a try. If I go bust, I can always come back here."

"If you can, you can," replied Pep. "You gonna tell Miss Sally? She's grown fond of ya, I can tell."

"Yep. I'll tell her tonight."

"So, when ya goin'?"

"With the mornin' sun."

After the evening meal was finished Sullivan walked back to the kitchen. He saw Sally Atkins cleaning the stove.

"Miss Sally, I need to tell ya somethin'."

"All right, Son. What's on your mind?"

"I'm leavin' in the morning."

"Oh. Oh my. Where are you headed?"

"I'm going to Texas."

"Texas? Oh my. Well a lot of people have done just that. If your head is set on that, then you go with my blessings, but I hate to see you leave. I'll miss you. Kinda got used to having you around."

"You been mighty good to me, and I appreciate it. But it's just time for me to move on. I been thinking about it for a long time."

"So, you got no family left here, right?"

"Right. My folks died before the war, long before. Nothing to hold me here. So why not just see what's over the hill and around the bend? It might be something good."

"I hope it is for you, real good."

"And like I say, thanks for all you did for me. When you have a chance figure up what I owe ya, and we'll settle up tonight. I'll be out and gone early in the morning."

"All right, Son," she said as she reached over and placed her left hand on his right cheek. "Would you mind if I ask you a personal question?"

"Why no, of course not."

"What you do is none of my business, nor what you ever did. But I just been concerned about you ever since that first night you were here. I just have felt there is something bottled up inside you, maybe some big kind of hurt that's eating away at you, and you never let it out. Always have heard it does a body good to talk. Do you have anything you need to say, talk about to get it out?"

"Why no, Miss Sally. I just went through the war like everbody else. Guess that tends to put a dent in ya that still hangs on a long time."

"Well, all right. But if you need to tell me anything at all you don't have much time left. Just thought I would offer."

"Thanks, Miss Sally. I do appreciate it."

Sullivan settled down in his bed for his last night in Atlanta. He wondered if he was doing the right thing. Not many people seemed to agree with him. But he would never know if he did not try, and . . . .

He heard her voice calling his name. It was clear and plain and irresistible. Then he saw her down the road and felt drawn to her in the old ways. He could not hold back, nor did he want to for he had lived for only one thing and that was to make it home to her. And now here she was, full of life and laughter and love . . . .

He was awakened early the next morning by a cock crowing a couple of houses over. Sullivan tried to slip out the front door, but stopped on the porch when he heard Miss Sally behind him say, "I fixed you a lunch and a little food you can eat on the way."

"Thanks, Miss Sally. I'll never forget ya."

"You do and I'll come to Texas and haunt you."

She leaned up and kissed him on the cheek, and said, "If you are ever back this way and need a bite to eat, you know where I am."

Sullivan smiled at her and walked away.

5

As he rode down the main street of Marshall, Texas Toombs Sullivan saw on the right side a large sign that read, Marshall Saloon and Cafe. Just what I'm looking for, he said to himself. He pulled up and tied his horse to a post. He stepped up on the wooden sidewalk, took his hat off and slammed it against both legs, watched the dust as it flew away, then went inside and found the place half full.

There was loud piano music and laughter and loud conversations. He could smell the food and the aroma of coffee and whiskey all mixed together. He saw an assortment of people, the kind of people he had never seen before. They were mostly a rough looking crowd, though there were a few who were a little more refined. He took them to be proper town folk who perhaps owned businesses. They were fairly well dressed. There were also a few women sitting around, and one attempting to sing as a man played the piano. The rest of the men were war veterans like him he assumed. Some still wore a hat or a shirt from the war. Still others must be cattle drivers, he thought. Most all of them had guns on them, pistols from the war or ones they had since purchased.

When he stepped up to the bar and laid his rifle against it, the bartender said, "What ya need, Mister?"

"I need a lot of things, but I'll have a whiskey to start."

The bartender poured him a drink, but before he could pick it up, he saw a man further down the bar draw out his pistol and say to the next man, "Harry Drew, you're under arrest. I'm a Texas Ranger, and I'm taking you to Austin."

Suddenly a man from the left came charging up behind the Ranger with a knife in his hand. As he was about to stab him Sullivan pulled out his pistol and shot the man in the back. The Ranger turned around, ducked somewhat and stepped slightly sideways as Harry Drew pulled out his pistol. Sullivan shot him almost between his eyes. Two dead men lay on the floor with the stunned Ranger standing between them. Sullivan crammed his pistol back under his belt, picked up the glass and drank down the shot of whiskey.

"Thanks, Mister, whoever you are."

"Don't like back-stabbing."

"I don't either, especially my back. Who are you?"

"Name's Toombs Sullivan."

"I'm Oliver Springtown," the Ranger said as he stuck out his hand. "Let's sit over there at a table."

The two men shook hands, Sullivan picked up his rifle, and they walked to a table against the far back wall and sat down.

Oliver Springtown was almost six feet tall and was of a heavy build. He had a dark complexion, brown hair, thick eyebrows, and a mustache that curled around the edges of his mouth. He wore a leather short coat, a vest under it, a dark blue shirt, and brown pants tucked into his high boots. His pistol, a Navy revolver, was in a holster high on his belt, waste high. He wore a wide-brim tan colored hat.

"How about I buy you a steak dinner? I owe you a favor."

"Fine with me. What about your two friends lying there on the floor?"

"They don't need anything. They already ate. Lead. Not my friends, of course. The bartender will send for the local sheriff, and he'll have them taken care of. I know the sheriff here, so there's no problem. I was after Drew, but the other one I don't know. A friend of his I would suppose. Where you from? John, two steak dinners!"

"I'm from Georgia."

"Ya been here long?"

"About five minutes."

"Newly arrived then. What brings you to Texas?"

"What brings anyone to Texas? I wanted to see it and find something here."

"What are you looking to find?"

"I don't know yet."

"You got any employment? You want to work with cattle? You teach school? You build houses? What?"

"I don't know. Do I look like a school teacher?"

"What you shoot in that rifle of yours, flats?"

"Yep, flats. They do the job."

"I can give you a job, since you seem to be qualified for a certain kind of work."

"What kind of work?"

"Being a Texas Ranger. I'm not usually alone when I come after somebody. I sent my men off chasing after some Comanches the other day. They stole some cattle, and so I came on here alone. We can always use another good man."

"How do ya know I'm a good man?"

"I saw you in action. I know what you can do."

"Tell me about your Comanches."

"They are the wildest, fiercest, and smartest Indians in the West. They can outride and outshoot and outfox and outrun anybody, and that includes the Army and us. Only we ain't gonna be outrode and outshot by them. That's why I can use a man like you."

"So, what is it they do that makes you want to outshoot them?"

"They raid and kill and rape and pillage and burn. They are stealing a lot of cattle. The problem is they steal the cattle, and then they sell it or trade with the Comancheros, another wild bunch of whites, Mexs, breeds. Then the Comancheros sell the cattle to government buyers who then send them to the Army. And that is back to the army many times. The army has bought back cows with their own brands already on them. And then we have your normal killers and robbers and bandits like Drew there, God rest his soul. He killed a man in Austin over a card game."

"Sounds like you have your hands full, Mister Springtown."

"More than full. That's why I need a man like you."

"All right, I'll sign on for a time and we'll see how this goes. But I don't know nothing about the law. I wouldn't know a bad man if I saw one."

"We are the law. We say if a man is a bad man or a bad Indian. And all the Indians are bad Indians. The only good Indian is one that has already gone to be with his fathers. Don't you want to know what it pays?"

"A man with no job don't care about what it pays. So far the food is free."

"Here's yore steaks, Boys. Bread will be right out. How about some beer to wash it down with?"

"Two, and thank ya, John."

As they began cutting into the steaks, Springtown said, "Now we need to go over to the store and get you outfitted for the job and the place. I'll advance you some money from that pay you don't care about."

"What do I need?"

"I saw that knife in yore boot. You need a Bowie knife in ya belt also. You need boots that are suited for Texas. Them you wearing ain't. You need leather chaps to protect yore legs. We go through rough country that's got briars and stickers and needles and thorns five inches long. You need a leather short coat, a vest like mine, and a slicker for rain. We have bad storms out here. You can get a long coat for the winter down in Austin later. You need a hat."

"I got a hat, as you can see."

"It's a fine hat."

"My father gave it to me before the war."

"You need a hat for Texas or you'll burn up, a wide hat."

"Here's ya beer and bread."

"Thanks, John," Springtown said.

"Yeah, thanks," Sullivan added.

In a moment Sullivan said, "What's all this gonna cost me?"

"It don't matter to you. Eat up."

Sullivan ate quicker than Springtown, so he pulled out his pistol and laid it on the table. He took two paper cartridges which contained powder and ball from a small bag he wore over his shoulder on his right side, placing one in one of the cylinders. He pulled down the packing lever from under the barrel and pressed it in tightly. Then he repeated that for the other empty cylinder. After that he placed an igniting cap on the nipple of each cylinder.

He looked up at Springtown and said, "It pays to be ready." Then he stuck his pistol back under his belt.

"Yes, it does," Springtown replied with a wry smile. "So, where you from?"

"Georgia. I got home and there weren't that much left, so I come out here after working in Atlanta a year."

"Where did ya get that rifle?"

"Off a Yankee who gave it up voluntarily."

"How so?"

"I had to kill him first. After that it was easy."

"So, you got to keep it?"

"I saw it was over. I didn't wait around for a surrender and all that. I just left early and went on back home. I had done what I could, and I didn't see no reason to prolong things. The war was done and I was done."

"Well, I stayed until the end. Some of these boys in the Rangers were there with me. I was a Major, and I could not leave the men. So, I stayed, but I didn't want to."

They continued to talk about the war and all they had experienced. But now, they agreed, it was over, over and done with it. It was time now to forget it and be one country again.

When they had finished their meal, Springtown paid for it, Sullivan picked up his Henry rifle, and they walked out the door. They crossed the street and went in a store where Toombs Sullivan became a Texas Ranger, at least in appearance that is. After that they checked into the hotel for a night's rest before the long ride to Austin.

6

The next morning the two men rode out of town headed south-west to Austin.

"I been a little surprised," Sullivan said.

"At what?"

"The large number of slaves, well, former slaves now, and the amount of cotton grown here."

"This area produced a lot of cotton. Yore people from Georgia, Carolina, Alabama came over here. They bought land, cheap land, planted a lot of cotton. They brought their slaves with'em. There's more of'em here and between here and Austin than any other part of the state. I don't know what will happen to them now. Did you and yore family own slaves?"

"Nope. No cotton grown up there in north-west Georgia, so nobody needed'em. Lots of people up our way were against the war. A county over the mountain never left the Union."

"It's cotton and cattle out here. Some people got fairly well rich on both or either that is. Nobody raises both at the same time. The one defeats the other. Don't know what will happen to cotton now, but the cow is king."

"You born here or what?"

"Nope, back in twenty-six. My folks came here from Tennessee when I was a kid. My father was chasing a dream. He had a farm back home, but knew there was lots of land here a man could get. I still remember when we crossed the Mississippi. It was like jumping into the unknown. Pa got all heated up after the Alamo and fought with Sam Houston. They didn't do too good with the ranch, but got by. Then one night the Indians came and burned us out, killed my folks. They hid me down the well. I grew up with a family back closer to civilization. That's why I joined up with the Rangers when I was eighteen. Been fighting Indians ever since. Then the war came along, and here we are. When I got back here a year ago I came back in the Rangers and got my old job back, along with some of the boys I had before."

"I guess you have seen some stuff, bad stuff."

"Yeah, but I don't know which is worse the war or what we have here. I will say being a Ranger prepared us for the war. And we felt like we was fightin' for our lives, just like we had been here."

"I can understand that."

On they rode with the rising sun mostly at their backs, saying nothing for a while.

Then Springtown said, "When we get to Austin, I'll introduce you to our boss, Major Henderson Pendergrass. He'll swear you in. I think you'll like him, good-natured but at the same time all business."

"Major, eh. So, what are you?"

"I'm a Captain."

"Captain of what?"

"Captain of a company."

"Captain of a company. Just like the army?"

"Nothin' like the army. I have fourteen men under me. We cover a wide range of territory, anywhere the Major wants us to go. We have side-arms, as you can see. I carry a Navy Colt, like most of the men. Some of them have the Army like you. We do most of our business with the Henry rifles we all have. The pistols are for short up-close situations."

"What do the people have you go after?"

"People like Drew back there have everything, pistols like ours, derringers they stuff down in their belts or boots, knives of all kinds, rifles like ours. The Indians have old flint-lock muskets, .58 caliber Springfield muskets, rifles from the war they took off whites they killed, pistols, knives, tomahawks, bows and arrows, and spears, and yeah, rifles like ours."

"Sounds dangerous."

"Everything and everybody in Texas in dangerous."

Three days later they arrived in Austin headed straight to Ranger headquarters and the office of Major Henderson Pendergrass. Austin, like Marshall, was a town of several thousand people. The difference was Austin was the state capital and as such took on an air of respectability and importance that Marshall lacked. Marshall was the jumping off place, Austin was one of the places to which new settlers jumped, if not for good at least they passed through looking for their destinies.

As they walked in Ranger headquarters Springtown said, "Major, I got a new man and I want him in my company since I recruited him. This is Toombs Sullivan."

Henderson Pendergrass was a tall man with broad shoulders and a look of authority. He was dark from the sun and held his head to the left side somewhat. He had a mustache which was dark, but there were little specks of gray appearing in his hair along the side of his head. He had been in charge of the Rangers for nearly five years before the war, having been a veteran of that agency for fifteen.

Major Pendergrass stood up and walked around to the front of his desk as he said, "Nice to meet you, Sullivan.

Welcome to Austin and to the Texas Rangers. You think you are qualified for this job?"

"Well, yes, Sir. I suppose I am."

"Is he Captain?"

"Yes, Sir, he is. He's the only reason I'm here today. If it weren't for him, I never would have been able to leave Marshall. He disposed of Drew and a friend of his before they could dispose of me. So, yes, yes, he's qualified. I have seen him in action."

"You caught up with Drew?"

"Yes, Sir. He wasn't hard to find."

"Where were your men? And where are they now?"

"On the way to Marshall we got word from a rancher that some Comanches had stolen his cattle and headed west. I sent them after them and went on to Marshall alone."

"And what have I told you about being alone? Cattle or no cattle, no more of that, Captain. You at least take a couple of men with you if that kind of thing happens again. Got it?"

"Yes, Sir, I got it."

Pendergrass turned around, picked up a Bible off his desk and held it out to Sullivan.

"I'll give you the short Pendergrass version. Put yore hand on this Bible. Do you swear to uphold the laws of the State of Texas and the United States of America and obey all commands of yore superior officers, so help you God?"

"I do."

"Congratulations, Son. You're a Texas Ranger."

Then Pendergrass walked back around behind his desk, opened a drawer, pulled out a badge, went back in front of Sullivan, penned it on his vest, and said, "Wear this badge with pride at all times."

"I will."

"Captain, let me know what yore men say when they get in here."

"Yes, Sir, I will. Will that be all?"

"Yep. I'll have something for you to do when they get here and rest up a bit. You two take it easy for a couple of days."

Springtown and Sullivan left the building and walked two blocks to the boarding house where Company D kept their permanent rooms.

Major Pendergrass sat at his desk and thought about this new man. Being in charge of the lives of men was a heavy responsibility he bore. It was an honor, but yes, a burden for he sent them off to die sometime just like he had in the army during the war. What would become of Sullivan and any of them for that matter? He tried not to think about such things. It would only weigh him down and interfere with his duties.

7

Three days later, late in the afternoon, Company D came back to Austin. When they walked in the boarding house they were met by Springtown and Sullivan.

They were a hard-looking bunch. That was Sullivan's first thought when he saw them. They looked like they had been riding hard, living hard, fighting hard. He knew he did not look like them, and wondered how he would fit in with them and whether they would accept him.

"Boys, we got a new man. This is Toombs Sullivan. I'll introduce the men to ya, Toombs. This is Sergeant Pete Blankenship, Johnny Brown, Jack McAllister, Bill Blount, Ned Crawford, Pete Rincon, Billy McCary, Andy Wilford, Willard Boyd, Blacky White, George Washington Smith, Ransom Pride, Willie Smart, and C. W. Pickles."

At first Sullivan had a bewildered look on his face, and then he smiled. The men laughed.

"Don't worry, Kid," Sergeant Blankenship said, "You'll learn our names as we go along. Sometimes we forget them, but nobody cares or gives a rip."

Then the men filed past Sullivan, shook his hand, and said welcome in several ways. They were a mixture of what Sullivan had already seen in Texas. They were tall and short, skinny and stout, and were all dirty and dusty, wearing evidence of a long trip. They were all dressed in the same way as he and Springtown with big hats, kerchiefs around their necks, vests bearing their badges, loose shirts, their pants tucked down in their high boots, gun belts at their wastes with only a couple of them without holsters. Those two pushed their pistols down under their belts the way Sullivan did. Almost every one of them had a mustache, with a couple of them having hair on their chins. They all seemed friendly enough and there was an obvious bond between them, like the one he had known in the war where you trusted your life to the men on your right and left. When he had met them all a silence fell over the room.

Springtown then asked, "All right, what happened?"

Being the second highest in rank, Sergeant Pete Blankenship always spoke for the group when it came to sharing information. He was a rough looking man with a full face bearing a couple of scars, whether from the war or fighting Indians, Sullivan did not know. It was not the kind of thing you asked a man about. He had a head full of brown hair, bushy eyebrows, and a little stubble on his face, for he did not like to shave.

Blankenship replied to the Captain's question, "Cap'n, by the time that rancher found us and said what happened those Indians had been gone several days. We followed their tracks all right, but then they split up and went in several directions. Weren't no way we could catch up with'em. They was just gone."

"I'll let the Major know about it. He'll have something for us, I know. Let's wash up and eat up."

Thirty minutes later the men were seated around the supper table, passing bowls and platters.

Blankenship asked Sullivan, "You from where?"

"Georgia."

"Marching through Georgia. Old Sherman did a dirty deal to that state. But we was on our last leg anyway. You leave family behind? Married back in Georgia? Got a wife?"

"No, never married. Folks been gone for years now. Nothing to hold me there, so here I am."

"I think all of us are Texans. We fought everywhere though. I guess you did as well."

"Yep. Everywhere."

"We was at Gettysburg. We did our best, but that was about the end of it in a way. The handwritin' was on the wall after that."

"Yep. That was it. I loved my state and fought for it, but I just couldn't stay there no longer. I came out here lookin' for I don't know what, but here I found this."

"Divine intervention," said Ned Crawford, "either that or the devil to pay. Don't know which, but like us you'll find out. If the Indians don't get ya the devil will."

"Ya better off if it's the devil that gets ya. All he'll do is burn ya up. The Indians do a lot of other stuff before they burn ya," said Bill Blount, as he laughed out loud. The other men laughed also.

Then Ned Crawford said, "Yep, them Indians are masters at killin' people the slow way. They like to drag it out. First, they'll tie ya down with stakes, stretch ya out or either they'll string ya up on a tree limb. I think the skinnin' is done real slow. Is that right, Boys?"

The men laughed again as Andy Wilford said, "Yep, real slow."

"After they skin ya then they take a sharp knife, thank God it's sharp, and they will cut yore private parts right off. Then they stick that knife in yore stomach low and cut you all the way up, and stuff yore private parts in yore mouth. Ya hair is the last thing to go. They give you a haircut, but by then ya generally don't mind one way or the other. Then after all that they'll cut you up in little pieces and feed you to their ponies. Anything that's left they leave for the wild animals around there. Often times they'll take yore head and put it on the end of a spear and ride back into their camp and show you off. The Indian women really like this part. Then they have a game where they line up and kick yore head around on the ground like you was some kind of ball or somethin'. Eat up young man, ya food'll get cold."

The men laughed, and then amid the clanking of forks on dishes broke into several conversations.

Toombs Sullivan listened closely to as many of those conversations as he could, first one and then another, trying to learn what he could. He heard bits and pieces.

"Skinned'em alive that day . . . ."

"They stole all of them and . . . ."

"We chased them for days that time, remember . . . ."

"After that I was ready to take some scalps myself . . . . Caught three of'em . . . . Shot him in the gut the first . . . ."

After nearly an hour the eating and the talking both died down about the same time. It was as though the men knew when to stop their conversations and begin listening. Captain Springtown stood up at the end of the long table.

"All right, Boys, the Major has something for us. There's been a number of apparent Comanche raids down south-west of here. Probably not that same bunch ya'll was trying to chase down. Company F is already down there looking around, but they might need some help. Reports indicate there might be three or four hundred Indians in that band of killers. We'll leave here in the morning. Bring all your guns, ammo, the usual stuff for a long trip out. Don't know how long we'll be gone. Sergeant, you be sure a couple of the boys get the pack mules ready. Ned, I want you to help Sullivan get a bed-roll, blankets, everything he needs. He's got none of that stuff, being new. Sullivan, you follow these boys around and do what they do and act like they act, most of the time that is, and act like you know what you're doin' and soon you will. Any questions from anybody? All right, better get some rest. We'll leave as early as we can, knowing we got to get things packed up."

As they got up from the table Ned Crawford walked over to Sullivan and said, "Well, Sir, you 'bout to jump right in it. Nothin' like the baptism of fire."

"I might as well start off with a bang."

"Stick close to me, especially if we run up on those Comanches. It'll be like fighting Yankees in a way, except they never wanted to cut your hair clean off your head. Let's step outside for a smoke."

As they went out on the wood plank sidewalk, they passed by a man sitting against the wall. He wore a Mexican sombrero and was wrapped in a blanket. He was slumped over with his legs crossed and his head down. After they walked past him, Sullivan looked back.

"Who was that sittin' there?"

"Oh, that's Joe Joe Buffalo. He's a breed of some sort, part Indian, part Mexican, and part white they say. He hangs around some, but he's harmless. Pay him no mind."

8

Texas Ranger Company D rode out of Austin late in the morning headed south-west in search of Camanches and hoping to meet up with Company F, which had been out for a couple of weeks. The fifteen men were in two side by side columns with Captain Oliver Springtown out front a lot of the time. At other times he had one of the Rangers riding point out ahead of them. At those times Sergeant Pete Blankenship pulled up beside him.

The heat was already rising by the time they had left town, and with the early afternoon it had soared. Dust from the horses rose around them. There was not a cloud in the bright blue sky, and there was no hope of any relief from the rays of the sun. Everywhere the grass was brown, having been parched by the sun and dying of thirst.

Ned Crawford and Toombs Sullivan rode side by side. At times they talked, and at other times nothing was said.

Crawford was a thin man of medium height. He had a bony face with sharp features, and a mustache that curled around the corners of his mouth, like several others including Springtown. His mouth was full of large white teeth and drew attention, almost making those he spoke with forget about the mustache.

He was a friendly sort, as were the others, but he seemed to be drawn to Sullivan, partly because Springtown had commanded him to look out for him, but also because he naturally liked him.

After a couple of hours Sullivan asked, "Where are the trees? I'm not seeing any real trees, not what I call trees."

"Those trees you're talking about are back in Georgia. Not much of that down in this part of the state."

"The Captain told me a little about these Comanches. What can you tell me about them?"

"Did he tell ya they're mean and dangerous killers?"

"Yes, he did."

"Well, double whatever he said."

"That'd be pretty bad."

"They are. It's like they have a chip on their shoulders, every dang one of them. We can thank them in a way, because they were so fierce years back that they kept the Spanish from coming on up further into Texas. Now they resent us being here because they have thought all along that this country is theirs, and they don't like to share nothin'."

"What do they look like? How will I know'em when I see'em?"

"Oh, you'll know'em all right. They dress in a variety of ways. Lots of times they wear no shirt, just leather pants they make and leather moccasins. Then at times they wear white man's clothes they either steal or take off the whites they kill or buy somewhere. Sometime they wear fine leather boots. They have money, like money a lot. They get it trading cattle, selling cattle to Comancheros."

"The Captain told me about that."

"They're very smart. They live in bands, groups, but not what you'd call a tribe, unless you think of all of them as a great tribe. Usually they have at least one, or more maybe, who speaks English and Spanish, as well as several other Indian languages. They go to trade fairs and buy and sell. They take stuff there they had stolen from whites and sell it or trade it for other stuff. Each band has its own leader, and sometimes those bands will join together, maybe two or three of them, and go on a war party after somebody or something. That's what we have with this large group we hope to find, several hundred together, but they won't be for long."

"I take it they move around a lot."

"They do. They live in tepees, you know, poles and some kind of cover, like tents."

"Yeah, I saw a picture one time."

"That way they can pick up and be gone before you can say Robert E. Lee."

"That's pretty quick."

"The best known amongst them are the Penatekas, or honey eaters, and the Quahadies or the buffalo eaters, and the Yap-eaters, because they eat yap, which is a plant with a root. I don't know which ones we'll be finding, if we find them at all. Now, I need to tell ya they got a fair grudge against us whites. Back in eighteen and forty there was this big meetin' with them. Thirty-three chiefs came together to talk with us whites, maybe to make peace. It was in a house where they all met, and so it's called the Council House Fight, because there was a fight, but not much of a fight. I don't know what happened, ain't sure nobody really knows, but somethin' went wrong and they broke out into a fight of some sort and all those chiefs were shot dead right then and there. They was supposed to bring in all their white captives, but only brought one woman. Maybe a deal could have been worked out, but it weren't. Well, you can imagine what happened. That all led to a bad time of raids. They raided the towns of Victoria and Linnville, down south-east of San Antonio, burned them to the ground, killed people, and stole horses and everything they could carry away. They was caught up with at a place called Plum Creek.

"When the Comanches left Linnvile they had stolen about two thousand horses, which is what they value more than anything else. Buffalo Hump was their leader. The people in Linnville escaped by getting in boats and going out on the water. It's a town down on the coast.

"Well, whites went after them and they weren't hard to catch trying to keep them horses and their women and children and all they stole all together. But the whites made a mistake and got off their horses, and then the Comanches, the best horsemen in the world, came at them and it was bad.

"At Plum Creek some time after that they was caught up with again, and again the whites got off their horses to fight the Indians who always circle around their enemy. But a couple of men kept urging them to mount up again and charge, and that turned the tide of that battle.

"Amongst those whites, all of whom were great shots and loved fighting Indians, was a man named John Coffee Hays, and he became the greatest Texas Ranger of them all. You see, these young men were adventurers, the likes of which them Indians had never run into. Lots of them was killed by the young whites."

"Must have been a heck of a fight."

"That ain't even the half of it. They fought them Indians for over fifteen miles, a runnin' battle. At one point them Camanches stopped long enough to kill their captives, and among them was a woman named Nancy Crosby. She was Daniel Boone's granddaughter. They tied her to a tree and shot her full of arrows."

"My God."

"Yeah. Here comes Johnny Brown. Let's gather up and see what he found out."

By the time Brown reached the Rangers they had all assembled near Captain Springtown so they could hear what was being said. Brown slowed from a gallop and pulled up his horse.

"Cap'n, they's a house over yonder about three mile off, beyond that rise. I didn't go on down thar, but things look normal to me."

"Thanks, Johnny. Okay Boys, let's go see what we can learn from those folks."

In a few minutes they were slowing up as they approached the house and saw a man come out of his barn with a pitchfork in his hands. He leaned the pitchfork against the barn and waved as a sign of welcome.

"You be Rangers."

"We are. I'm Oliver Springtown."

"Get down, get down. Ya'll can water yo horses ov'ar."

"Thanks. We're out lookin' for Comanches. Seen any?"

"Naw. If they'd a come by here you wouldn't be talkin' to me now. You'd be looking at a pile of ashes and me hung up some place drying in the sun. My woman wouldn't be here neither."

"We know they're down here some place. Another company of Rangers came this way. Seen 'em?"

"Oh yeah. Weeks back. They was lookin' for the same Indians I reckon."

"That'd be them."

"It's gettin' on toward the sinkin' of the sun. If you wanna camp here of an evenin' you can."

"That'd be mighty nice of you. I think we will."

"Help yo'self to water, feed in the barn. I'll tell the wife to cook up some extra, well, a lot extra."

"Say, when do we come to another home place?"

"My neighbor's on down thar 'bout ten mile. Name of Claxton. I'm Jim Boutwell, wife is Jesse."

"Pleased to meet ya and thanks for the hospitality."

9

The next morning the Rangers and their horses were well fed and well rested. Each Ranger thanked the Boutwells, and then they headed off to find the Claxton place. It was another hot and dusty day.

Toombs Sullivan was beginning to get a feel for the land and the people he had encountered, though it was mostly Rangers so far. They had taken him in graciously and made him feel like he belonged from the first moment he met them. He felt like he had learned a lot in only a few days.

He had learned more than he wanted to know about the Comanches, and did not want to know more, not first-hand at least.

As they began their journey for the day, Sullivan wondered what he had gotten himself into. He decided his problem was he did not know why he had even come to Texas. He had not come to find anything in particular, just Texas.

He had not come to find riches, and it was a good thing because he had not seen any. Maybe he had come to find adventure and excitement. He was about to find more of that than he wanted, and had already experienced enough of both in the war. He just jumped at the first job that had been offered to him, since he was in the habit of eating meals at regular intervals, and he had about used up all the money he had just getting to Texas. He was beginning to understand he had not really come to find anything at all. He had come in order to run away from what he already had, a dead wife and son and a burned down house and barn on a dirt farm. The Yankees had promised the slaves forty acres and a mule. He had already had both and he could tell them there was not much to either, not enough to get enthusiastic about. The Indians, these crazy killers, Ned had certainly opened his eyes about them. If he had known all that he had told him he might still be back at that saloon in Marshall instead of out here offering up his fine head of hair for auction.

His thoughts were suddenly interrupted by Captain Springtown, "George Washington, take the point!"

G. W. Smith rode off at a gallop ahead of the rest of them. G.W. is what all the Rangers called him. Only the Captain used his first and middle names.

"So, you was in the war like the rest of us," Ned Crawford said.

"Yeah, I was. I did my duty because I had to, just like you and everybody else who could walk and carry a gun."

"We should have won that war, could have won it easy. I ain't never got over it. Think about it all the time I ain't talkin', and I talk about it a lot even then. Things ain't never gonna be the same again. We lost something. I never owned no slaves, and never knowed nobody who did. But some in Texas did. I guess they wanted to keep them too. For me it was all about politicians in Washington tellin' the rest of us what we had to do. That's why I fought, and I would fight again if we ever get the chance."

"I didn't go fight for any reason at all. I went because the state of Georgia was in it. And we all was called to go, all of us of an age. I never thought about why I was there. I just was that's all. But when I saw it was over, I was over. I left before it really ended and headed home. I walked all the way from Virginia to Georgia. You think I was wrong for doin' that?"

"Nobody who did anythin' in that war or at the end, during it, or after it was wrong. We all did what we had to in order to survive. I don't blame you one bit. You alive ain't ya?"

"Yep, I am."

"That's good enough."

About an hour later Smith came riding back to the column, and said loud enough for everyone to hear him, "Captain, up ahead there's a burned-out home place. I didn't go on down to it, but it looks pretty bad."

"It must be the Claxton place", the Captain said. "All right, Men, let's go take a look."

They moved along at the same speed as before, not all that slowly, but not at a gallop. They needed to save the strength of the horses in case they needed it later. Besides, there was no hurry in getting there. The damage had already been done.

When they came in sight of the little ranch, they could see the home and the barn had both been burned almost down.

As they drew closer, they could see five bodies. There was a man who had been nailed to the side of the barn, what was left of it. He was completely nude, his clothes obviously torn away from him in a violent way. They had taken his scalp, the dried blood parched on his face. They had skinned him from his navel up to his neck, probably while he was still alive, as was their custom. Then they cut off his genitals and stuffed them in his mouth.

The woman, who was obviously his wife, had been stripped of her clothing, raped probably several times, her throat cut, and her scalp taken. They cut her abdomen open in case there was a baby there.

There were three teenage boys, all of them scalped, partially skinned, and stretched and tied out on the ground with the ropes tied to pegs. Their genitals were also in their mouths.

"Okay, Boys, you know what to do."

The men looked around and found a couple of shovels and picks. They began digging graves.

"Sullivan, you come with me. Let's look at what's left of this house."

They walked in where there had been a front door, and Springtown pushed away a couple of burned rafters.

"See what you can find, so we'll know what they took and if there was anybody else here."

They both kicked around in the ashes and what was left of furniture. In a few minutes Sullivan found something.

"Captain, look at this."

He held up a dress he had found. The Captain came over and took it.

"This looks like it would fit a girl of maybe ten or twelve years old. That means they took her with them, since we didn't find her lying out there. This is what they do, Sullivan."

"What will happen to her?"

"Most likely she'll become a member of a family. When she gets a little older, she'll be the wife of one of them. Unless she is rescued by somebody, she'll become an Indian woman. Some of them girls would not come back to the whites if they had the chance."

"Why?"

"They grow into it. They live with the Indians a while, and they adopt their ways over time. They become what their new family is. That's most of them, I think. Of course, some of them would come back and be glad, but not most I don't think. Let' go see how the boys are doin'."

They walked out of the charred ruins of the house and found the others over near the barn, between it and the house.

"How's it goin'?"

"We'll be through diggin' in a while, Captain," replied Sergeant Pete Blankenship. "Then the hard part, bringing them over here and puttin'em in the ground. They just about rank."

"They're past that, Pete. Well, do what you can, and we'll say some words."

An hour later the repulsive but necessary task was completed. Captain Springtown pulled out a small Bible from his saddlebag, read a Psalm, and said a prayer.

Then he said to the men, "Well. That does it. Let's go see if we can find'em."

There being no tracks to follow, they rode south hoping to find some sign of the Comanche band that hit the Claxtons. After a few miles they stopped. The Captain turned half way around in his saddle.

"Blacky, Ransom, Andy, the three of you ride on ahead and spread out wide. See if you can find anything."

The three men rode off at a gallop, as Captain Springtown called out, "Awright, let's go. Crawford and Sullivan, you take the mules for a while now."

"Right, Captain," Crawford said.

He and Sullivan moved to the back of the column and each of them took a rope from a mule. The mules were sometime cooperative and sometime ornery. Sometime they moved quietly along and sometime they bellowed out their protest.

"Come on!" Crawford said. "A good kick in the ass will get ya movin' if I have one bit of trouble out of you."

10

For the next three days they rode south, with Springtown sending riders ahead south, east, and west, but they never found a trace of the Comanche band. One day at mid-afternoon they came to the Nueces River.

"We'll stop here and rest up, camp for the night," called out Captain Springtown. "Water yore horses first thing. Then water yoreselves and bathe if ya like. Some of ya need it."

The men dismounted and led their horses to the edge of the river where they let them drink. Then they tied them off back away from the river, and took their saddles off them. They put their saddles and weapons several yards away from the horses, and undressed at the edge of the river. They waded in and sat down, putting their heads under the water.

"Man, this feels good," said Bill Blount. "I feel like I just lost about ten pounds of dirt and dust."

"I hope ya lost a few pounds of stink as well," replied Ned Crawford. "You needed to do that."

"Yeah, well you still smell like that mule you was leading even after gettin' in the river."

"Haw-hee-haw, hee-haw!"

"Mule head."

"You two love-birds shut up," said Sergeant Blankenship. "You'll upset the mules. When ya get through playing in the water unload those mules and get the food out for supper. And everything we need to cook it and eat it."

"Yes, Boss," answered Crawford.

"I'll help ya," Sullivan said.

Later in the evening Ransom Pride came back from searching in the west. About an hour later Wilford Boyd returned from the east. As the sun began sinking, Willie Smart still had not come back. He had gone across the river and southward.

"What ya think, Captain?" Sergeant Blankenship asked as they stood by a fire.

"I don't know. Right here is where he crossed the river, according to those tracks we saw over there. I assume they're his. He's been gone too long now. It wouldn't be smart to go out at night looking for him, but we'll get goin' in the morning. Maybe he'll be in before then."

The Rangers were up bright and early the next day along with the sun. They made coffee and ate what they had with them. No one said anything about Willie Smart, but their concern was written across their faces. He was the youngest of the Rangers, and was liked by all of them. It was his honesty, innocence, and trust in the rest of them that made him so well thought of. They had almost adopted him as their kid brother. He still looked like a boy, small and frail, sandy hair, and a ready smile. All of this made his not showing up even more of a concern.

"Awright! Five minutes and we'll be goin' on across the river," Springtown called out. "If ya got to take one, take it quick."

Several of the men hurried off behind trees. Others rolled cigarettes, lit up cigars, or put a plug of tobacco in their mouths.

Ten minutes later they saddled up, and approached the river's edge.

46

"Keep yore powder dry now!"

They eased their way into the river and came out on the other side.

"Ned, take the point!"

"Can I take Sullivan with me?"

"Nope. You know better than that."

"Right, Captain."

Ned Crawford rode off ahead of the others. He soon disappeared into the patch of Acacia trees beyond. The Ranger column followed slowly, in no hurry to cover ground that day. Springtown was concerned that they may be getting close to where the Comanches were, and he wanted to be careful as they advanced.

Toombs Sullivan was riding beside Andy Wilford now. He turned to him and asked, "What ya think?"

Wilford seemed to be a quiet man, speaking only when spoken to. He was short, had a mustache and goatee, and part of his face was pocked.

"I don't rightly know," Wilford replied. "You can expect anything down here in this country. Is there an Indian behind every tree? Not right now, I don't reckon, but there very well could be. Just keep yore eyes open and yore hand not far from yore gun. Just in case, that is."

"Sounds like good advice."

"It is good advice. It's why I'm still here. It was give to me by a man that ain't with us no more. Reckon he didn't take his own advice that day, and didn't keep his hand near his gun."

Wilford had grown up in New Orleans, the son of a merchant. With the war he had left home for the first time and he never went back. The war had done something to him, as it did to everyone else, but he could just never return to what life had been. There was a certain grimness to his face and his speech. It was almost like today could be his last day. Many days like that in the war had created that feeling he had and the outward expression of it.

Two hours later Ned Crawford came over the horizon at a gallop. In a couple of minutes, he pulled up his horse in front of Springtown.

"Captain, I found him. It's bad."

"Take us to him."

They rode as quickly as they could over a little rise and then for close to an hour before they saw Willie Smart lying on the ground. His horse was gone, as were his boots, his guns, his hat, and his scalp. He had been shot with three arrows and two bullets, likely from a rifle like they all carried with them. Whether it was his or one they already had, they did not know. They buried him in the shade of a tree, with Captain Springtown saying the words and the prayer.

"Well, Boys, we came here to find them, and I guess the Kid did. Makes me wonder about Company F. Where are they?"

It was close to noon when they saddled up again, as Springtown said, "Billy McCary take the point. Bill Blount and Johnny Brown, take it east and west. Forward, Men."

The further south they rode the hotter it seemed to be, the sun burning down on them. But in reality, it was hot where they had already been, hot everywhere. The dust rose and filled their mouths, noses, ears. They wiped away the sweat, now dirty looking from the dust. They were growing more and more concerned now about being ambushed by the Comanches, a favorite trick of theirs. No one spoke as they rode along. Their eyes were scanning all around, looking for any movement, anything that was unusual.

About mid-afternoon Billy McCary came back to them. He had found Company F.

"They're all dead, Captain. All of them. They been lying there for days, maybe weeks."

"Take us to them," Springtown said.

Soon they reached the place where Company F had been attacked. The men were lying fairly close together, making it appear they had dismounted to fight, always a mistake when facing Comanches. Their naked bodies had apparently swollen in the heat of the sun and burst open. They were discolored, skinned, heads cut off, eyes gouged out, genitals in their mouths, and scalped. Either wild hogs or coyotes had been eating them, maybe both. Once again, their clothing was missing along with their boots, hats, guns, and of course they took their horses.

"Captain, we got no shovels," said Sergeant Blankenship somberly.

"Yea, I know.... Pile them up and burn'em. Maybe we can cover over what's left. Dang savages. If we catch up to them, we'll kill everyone of'em."

As the men were disposing of the bodies, Springtown said to them, "We'll move on further south before we camp for the night. I don't think none of us want to be around here any longer than we need to be. Bill and Johnny will catch up to us. They'll know where we went."

When Johnny Brown came into their camp late in the afternoon, he reported he had seen no sign of Indians or anyone else. But Bill Blount had a different story to tell. When he came in later on, he jumped off his horse and rushed up to Captain Springtown.

"Captain, I found some of'em. They had cut east and are camped along the Dulce River. Looks like they been there a while and don't seem to be heading out anywheres."

"Tell us more."

"They're down in a low place along the river. There's lots of high banks and bluffs along it, ya know, but they're where there's some flat land. I crawled up on a little ridge and lay there watching them. We could sit up there and pick'em off before they ever knew what hit'em."

"How far away are they?"

"I'd say 'bout fifteen, eighteen mile away."

"How many ya think?"

"Oh, I say there was about forty or fifty in all, countin' women and children. There was no sign anywhere of the rest of'em, if there was a couple of hundred. Don't have no idea where they might of went. We could take'em easy."

"You come by where we found Company F?"

"I did. I could tell what most likely happened there. The smell is still in the air, the smell of death. I could see there was a fire. Figured what you'd done."

"Worst thing I ever saw."

"We can make'em pay, Captain."

"We will, and they'll pay a double portion for all their sins. Did you see the young white girl?"

"No sign of her. They must have sent her off with another group."

Later in the evening Toombs Sullivan sat by the fire with some of the other men. There was not much being said. Sullivan became lost in his thoughts. He had seen some horrors in the war, but nothing like what he had witnessed in these last several days. He had heard the word savage applied to Indians, but he had no idea what that was like or what it meant. Now he was beginning to understand. He was also beginning to understand the Rangers' hatred of the Comanches. What he had heard about them was beginning to be proven as true. And on the next day he knew he would be seeing what the Rangers did to pay the savages back a double portion.

11

The men gathered around Captain Springtown as they were about to head out. They held their horse's reins in their hands as they stood in a circle. Two of the men held to the mules.

The sun was rising quickly in the east, promising another scorching day. There was no breeze as yet, but each man hoped for one. Better still would be a light shower of rain, but there did not appear to be a cloud in the hazy unfolding sky.

"Awright, Men, we'll hit them at dawn in the morning. We won't be in no hurry to get there. Bill will lead us to the place where they're at, but we won't get close to'em. He'll sneak on ahead, take a look, and make sure they're still there. We'll camp, and be at that ridge he talked of just as the sun peeps up. Our goal is to kill them all. We need to let the women and children escape, but any man over the age of, say about fifteen, needs to be shot down dead.

As always check your ammo for once the shootin' starts there won't be no time to wonder. I say this mostly for you Sullivan. These other boys know this already, but then I guess you do too from the war and all. Okay, questions?"

There was a slight pause, and then Springtown said, "Okay, mount up."

As they began their journey, Sullivan wondered about what they were going to do. He understood the need of killing all the Comanche warriors for they should be punished and stopped from what they had been doing. The Rangers were there to protect and defend. He wanted to do that, but he did not know about killing fifteen year-old boys. Though he tried to never think about it, somebody had killed his son. But then maybe not. Maybe the boy and his wife had died of some sickness or maybe they starved to death. He would never know what happened to them. There was no one to ask. But killing . . . .

"What you so deep in thought about?" asked Ned Crawford, who was riding beside him.

"Oh, nothin' really. Just thinking about today and tomorrow."

"Well, don't worry about it. You'll get the hang of it.

Just aim and shoot. If they get on their horses, shoot the horse first. They're easier to hit, then kill the Indian. Hard to hit 'em when they're ridin' right at ya."

"I can imagine."

"Course, we'll be up on that hill, so the advantage will be to us. But I 'spect we'll have to go on down there and finish some of 'em off. Then we may need to see to the women and the children. Never know what they'll do or where they'll go. They may all jump in the river for all I know. Good riddance, I say. It's a wide flowing river. They'll wash on down soon enough."

"How many Indians have you killed?"

"I don't know. I never counted. How many Yankees did you kill?"

"I have no idea. I got my share, I guess. Never thought about counting. I think maybe I did for a while. But then I lost track. One battle kinda faded into the next at times. But then there were long times between some battles, and I didn't want to think about killin' then. I just wanted peace and quiet, which I never really found."

"I'd like to have some too if you two would shut up," said Andy Wilford.

"Oh, bite a cow's tail. We're tryin' to get sleepy too. Sometime ya got to talk things out and get in the mood. I'm tryin' to help the new man get into things here, ya know."

"Well, help him get into sleepy time."

Toombs Sullivan lay awake a long time looking at the stars and wondering what he was doing out there in the middle of nowhere. He thought about the coming battle, what they would do and how it might end. He had no qualms about shooting the Indians after what he had seen. That could not go unpunished. It was down-right uncivilized. If they did not stop those savages, they would continue to do the same thing over and over.

He had that uneasy feeling in the pit of his stomach, that churning and almost sickening feeling. He had experienced that a number of times before in the war. He was used to that and knew it would pass once the shooting started. But this time his thoughts were different. Before he had never faced the possibility of killing women and children, and my God, he thought, fifteen year-old boys. It was always very plain, very easy to see the enemy and pick them off one by one, but not this time. There would be no blue uniforms. They would all be running together. In the heat of it, in the midst of all that firing how could he tell the difference in men and women? If he could count the stars in the sky perhaps he could stop thinking about all this. They were so far away and yet out there in that country they were so close, close enough to . . . .

He saw fields of high grass with the wind blowing through them, high grass that would soon need to be cut for hay. The wind blew through the leaves and the limbs of near-by trees, and some of the leaves floated to the ground. He could see himself standing there by that field as he felt the wind slightly touching his face, and he saw his young son running toward him. And there was his wife following him, bringing him some water in a pitcher in one hand and she held a cup in the other. He saw her beautiful hands, hands that had not been scared by all the work she had done. And there was her beautiful auburn hair with the wind lightly blowing through it. There was, he was sure, never before such a beautiful . . . .

"Sullivan, wake up. We got to get going now."

"What time is it?"

"I don't know or care. It's Captain time. We got a ways to go now, and he said let's get at it. So, we will."

"All right."

The men got their gear together, saddled their horses, mounted up, and rode off toward the ridge. They took no time for eating anything, and certainly did not want to start a fire for coffee or anything else. Ned Crawford knew what Sullivan was thinking as they began to move out.

"We'll eat what the Indians were going to eat for breakfast. Might even be somethin' we can swallow down."

They rode hard for about fifteen minutes with Captain Springtown and Bill Blount out front. They began slowing down, then moved forward very slowly. They stopped and dismounted with all of them doing what they saw Springtown and Blount doing, tying their horses to scrubs. Then they pulled their Henry rifles out of their scabbards, pushed their pistols further down in their holsters or further under their belts, adjusted their hats, and then they looked at Springtown.

He placed one finger to his lips and waved them on, slightly crouching as he led them forward.

They moved quietly, low, and slow near the edge of the ridge. They crawled through the tall grass the last twenty feet in the weakening darkness. The grass felt cool to them. They lined up along the edge, all of them lying on their stomachs. They looked down toward the river and saw the Comanche camp, two rows of tepees, their horses tied at the far end of the camp, and a few cooking fires still smoking from the night before.

Sullivan was calm now, his hands steady, his eyes clear, his mind and senses alert. Suddenly he heard something behind him, running toward them.

"My God!" he said, almost screamed it out.

12

Sullivan had turned just in time to see the Comanche with a tomahawk raised up in his right hand and a knife in his left, and just in time to see Ned Crawford sink his Bowie knife into the Indian's stomach as he fell over both of them, blood gushing out. He heard the thud as the butt of Bill Blount's rifle crashed into the forehead of a second Indian. But the first had managed to scream out just as he fell forward. Blount then pounced on the other Indian with his knife.

That scream alerted the camp as the first rays of light fell down on it and the river, with the sun getting ready to come slowly up over the bluff on the other side of the river. Indians came pouring out of the tepees with their rifles in their hands. The Rangers could see many of them were wearing the clothing of the men in Company F. This only served to anger them and stiffen their resolve to kill them all.

"Let'em have it, Boys!" Springtown called out.

They began firing rapidly, dropping the Comanches in their tracks. Several made it to their horses, jumped up on them, and came charging at the Rangers. Up the ridge they came, screaming and shooting. Sullivan shot one horse, and then its rider as he jumped to his feet. The other four were also stopped in the same way.

It was over almost as quickly as it had begun. The Rangers walked slowly down the small hill and into the camp. They stood silently, looking all around. A couple of pistol shots rang out as they finished off some who had not been killed at first. They looked inside the tepees, making sure they were empty. A couple of Rangers went through the camp to where the horses were. Then they untied them and drove them away.

They looked at the dead Comanches. Some had on boots and others the coats or shirts of the Rangers. In their tepees they found hats and other clothing, as well as some personal items they had taken off the Rangers. They found their rifles and pistols and Bowie knives. They gathered up what they could take back with them.

The women and children had disappeared quickly, and no one cared where they went or what would happen to them.

Sullivan walked through the camp looking at all the dead bodies. He wanted to see every one of them since these were the first Indians he had any contact with. He looked at them closely, and rolled over any who were on their stomachs.

When Ned Crawford came up to him, he asked him, "Ned, are we going to bury them?"

Crawford smiled his toothy grin, spit out tobacco juice and said, "Heck no. Maybe the scalp hunters will hear of them and come down here and have their way with them. There's some fine looking hair here which they would love to have."

"Scalp hunters?"

"Oh yea, scalp hunters. They get twenty-five dollars for every one they bring in. If it's some bad Indian leader they can sometime get fifty for his scalp."

"Are you tellin' me the truth?"

"Sure I am."

"Who are these people?"

"They're white men like you and me. The Indians take our scalps and we take theirs. Seems fair to me."

"Well."

"They need to get here before these red warriors rot. But, of course, if they rot some the scalp comes off easier. But now I wouldn't want no rotten scalp. Too messy, and I ain't sure no one would pay for them anyway. Some of them will cut down and include both ears along with the scalp. I've seen them. Makes a fine presentation, if I do say so myself."

"All of this is new to me."

"Don't worry. You'll get used to it, this and a lot more."

"There's more?"

"You've only seen a little of what the Indians do to whites, and to each other for that matter. They are the most inventive people on God's good earth when it comes to ways of killin' and torturin' people. They do things me and you could never think of, would not imagine, and would not do them to anybody, not even to Indians."

"And I thought the war was bad."

They heard Captain Springtown call out, "Awright, Men, let's set these tepees on fire and pile on everything you can find that would be of any use to any Indian! Don't leave nothin' lying around. Where the rest of them went we can't say right now, but we'll find them, by jingo, we'll find them yet."

The Rangers began going to the open fires and taking pieces of burning wood from them. Then they went to all the tepees and set them on fire. They piled on bows and arrows, blankets, bowls, spears, tomahawks, knives (except for those they kept for themselves), skins, furs, and everything else they could see including their older rifles and pistols that were out of date.

When that was done, they brought their horses down to the camp. They made coffee and began eating some of what they had brought with them and some of the dried meat the Indians had. They did not know what it was, whether it was buffalo, deer, horse, or dog. They did not want to know. Some things are better to remain unknown.

When they finished eating their meal they began to wander off on their own for their private moments. Then one by one they came back to camp, undressed on the banks of the river, and went in the water. It had been a couple of days since they had cleaned up, though most all of them had back at the Nueces River. Still only a day in the dust and heat had made it necessary again.

By mid-morning they had begun their hot and dusty ride back to Austin. Though they had not found the larger band of Comanches, they at least stopped some of them. And they had found Company F. They were also low on supplies now, and that meant they had to go back.

Each man had a feeling of satisfaction, Captain Springtown most of all, every man but one. That man was Sullivan. While the rest of the men talked and laughed and told stories as they slowly rode along, Sullivan receded into himself.

He was unsure of what he felt. The experience was new and so were his feelings. It was not like the war at all. The killing of Indians was both easy and difficult. It was satisfying and disturbing. It was fulfilling and stressful. It made him proud and ashamed. He would never do it again, and could not wait for the next opportunity. He had nothing against the Indians, and hated every one of them. He would leave Texas and go further west or back to Georgia, and he would stay there the rest of his life. He would become a cattle rancher or a farmer, and he would always be a Ranger and nothing else. He would find another good woman and settle down and raise children, and he would never marry again.

"Where you at, Sullivan?" Crawford asked.

"I don't know."

13

Captain Oliver Springtown sat across the desk from Major Henderson Pendergrass and gave his report.

"They were all dead for days or weeks when we found them, dead and mutilated, the Comanche way. We burned the bodies and covered what was left as best we could. We had no way to bury them. The wild Indians even took their badges, I guess. We didn't see none. I reckon they're wearing them now. We never did see where they split up, but we took care of that band we did find at the Dulche River. We must'a kilt twenty, twenty-five or so. The women and their children went off some place we never did see. We burned all they had with them. And that's, that's about it, Major."

"All right, Oliver. So, how'd the new man work out?"

"He did just fine. He's a natural at this. He don't know it, but I think he is."

"I hate like everything we lost those good men. Captain Boykin was as fine a Ranger as we ever had. All of them were, well, you knew them."

"Yes, Sir."

"Sorry about young Willie. He was a good boy."

"He was. Among the finest."

"You know we cannot let this be. It can't go unpunished, not what was done to that family and to our men."

"No, Sir. We can't let it be, not like it is."

"You and your men take a few days off and rest up. Then I'll have a plan for ya."

"Right. Is that all?"

"That's it for now. Rest up. You're going to need to be rested for sure this time."

Springtown got up and walked out of the office and onto the wooden board sidewalk out front. He looked up and down the street. He had been back in Austin fifteen minutes, but he felt like he was still riding. He walked across the street to the saloon his men frequented often. He assumed they were there washing the dust out of their mouths. When he walked in, they were all standing at the bar, taking up most of it. When they saw him, they turned around, and Blankenship was the first to speak.

"What did the Boss say?"

"He said drink up while you can. Rest a few days, and then go after those Comanches again."

After a moment of silence, the Rangers returned to the conversations they had been having.

Joe Joe Buffalo sat at the table at the back of the room. Two of the Rangers sat down at a table near him. He never looked up. One of them said, "Hey, Joe Joe Buffalo."

Joe Joe Buffalo merely grunted and pulled out from under his blanket an empty whiskey bottle.

The other Ranger said, "Dumb drunk Indian."

When they got to their room that night Toombs Sullivan and Ned Crawford took their boots off first thing. Then they took off their belts, a holstered one for Ned and just the ammo belt Toombs was wearing. Ned stretched out on the double bed they would both sleep in, and Toombs sat down in the chair and propped up his feet.

"Well, now that we're back, what do ya think of yore venture out into the wild world of the Indian?"

Toombs thought a minute and then said, "I think it was wilder than I had imagined it would be. Back home in Georgia I never gave much thought to the west, to Texas, except that I knew it was out here. I knew there were Indians and all, but this is somethin' you can't imagine until ya see it. Then it don't even seem real at first. I kept thinkin' I'd wake up from a dream, a nightmare."

"Well, I grew up here. It's all in my blood. My folks came out here when I was a lad. That was back when Texas had just become a country. I never knowed anythin' else.

I couldn't live nowheres else. It wouldn't seem natural. Someday this place will settle down. The Indians, all of 'em, will make peace or we will kill all of them, and it don't matter to me which it is. But it'll be a safe place someday, a good place to be."

"Yeah, I guess that's true. It happened to all the other states comin' this way. So, civilization just has a way of movin' on west, and it'll get here more and more as time goes on. Just hope I live to see it."

"Oh, you will, Son, you will. . . . if the Comanches don't get ya first."

"Thanks."

Over the next three days the Rangers of Company D spent their time relaxing, eating, drinking, sleeping. They cleaned their weapons, restocked their ammunition, tended to their horses, cleaned up their saddles, walked up and down the streets of Austin, and tried not to think about going out again. A few of them looked for women.

Major Henderson Pendergrass spent the time devising a plan to punish the Comanche bands that had been running wild. It was a common thing to have cattle stolen, a ranch burned out, people killed. They did what they could to fight that. But wiping out a Ranger company, Company F, was one step too far. They had done it now, and this meant all out war.

On the third morning Major Pendergrass met with Captain Springtown, Captain Jacob Long of B Company, and Captain Jedidiah Trumbull of E Company, and explained what he had envisioned.

Oliver Springtown walked into the office, spoke to all three men who were there, and they all took a chair and sat down. The three Captains looked across the desk at Pendergrass. He looked tired out at the beginning of the day, as though he had been up all night pondering what to do. All three Captains noticed it, but neither of them had the nerve to say anything about his appearance.

"Here's what I want to do. See what ya think of this. I want companies B, D, and E to sweep south Texas. You leave here in two days time, not together, but spread ten mile apart. Move down to San Antonio where you will meet. Stay there one night, and see what you can learn, if anything. Then head out south again, about ten mile apart at all times. This way you can cover a lot of ground, but a rider can bring you all together fairly quickly if you should come upon somethin', either of the three companies. When you find those Comanches, if you do find them, then all three companies will attack. That'll give ya forty-five men bearing down on them. Hopefully you can catch more than just one band alone. Maybe you can catch a large group of them. That carries with it some danger, I know, but you will have them out-gunned for sure. You may just have to hunt down a band at a time. That means you'll be gone quite a while. So, prepare and take provisions for an extended stay."

"Sounds fine to me," said Jedidiah Trumbull.

The other two Captains nodded their heads in agreement.

"Any questions?" Pendergrass asked.

The three Captains looked at each other and back at Pendergrass, who said, "Good luck and God speed."

As they walked outside, they saw Joe Joe Buffalo sitting on the sidewalk, his back against the wall of the office. Captain Long nudged him with his boot, but he never looked up. He just grunted.

Long said to the other two, "Always drunk."

The next two days were spent getting ready, gathering supplies, cleaning weapons again, checking their ammunition, caring for their horses, resting, and eating good meals. Most of all they enjoyed sleeping in beds.

After supper on the last night, as they sat at the table after the others had left, Toombs Sullivan asked Ned Crawford and Blacky White, "How long you think we'll be out?"

"Hard to say," White replied. "Could be a couple of weeks or longer. Could be until we run out of supplies."

"How long would that take?"

"Hard to say."

Blacky White never said much, spoke seldom, and when he did speak, he was always noncommittal. He was a skinny man with a long neck and a protruding Adam's apple. His nose had a little crook in it. Some said it was broken during a fight with a Yankee soldier. Others said no, he was born ugly. Blacky White never said anything about it one way or the other. He figured it was his nose.

Sullivan turned to Ned Crawford for an answer to his questions, but got none.

"He's right," Ned said with a shrug. "Let's go get a drink. Or two."

The three men walked to the saloon across the street. Before they ever got there, they were met by loud piano music, laughter, boisterous talking, and when they went in the swinging doors, they smelled the smoke of cigars and the aroma of whisky. They stepped up to the bar.

"Three," Ned Crawford said.

Each man picked up a glass and drained it quickly.

"More," Crawford said.

When they had finished those he then said, "Let's go sit down." They took their empty glasses with them.

As soon as they were seated a man walked up to them.

"Hey, you three are Rangers they tell me. Would that be right?"

"That would be right," Crawford replied.

"You might be important now, back here in Texas, but we sure whipped your tails back east."

Ned Crawford stood up, pulled out his Colt Army pistol, and struck the man on the top of his head. When the man hit the floor, Crawford grabbed the collar of his shirt and dragged him to the door. Then he pulled him outside and rolled him into the street.

"You might've whipped our tail back east, but I just whipped yours right here in Texas. God bless Sam Houston."

Crawford walked back in and said, "A bottle, please."

When the bartender gave it to him, he walked over to the table. As he was about to sit down, the man he had thrown out came back in with his pistol in his hand. He pointed it at Crawford. Toombs Sullivan pulled his pistol from his belt and shot the man. He was dead before he landed on the floor.

Crawford got up, took hold of the man's shirt collar again, and pulled him back outside.

"Bet you'll stay out here this time."

When he sat back down, he looked over at Sullivan and said, "I understand you are pretty good at shootin' up saloons like this one. I'm glad."

14

Each company had five pack mules loaded down and also an extra horse. They carried with them tents, cooking pots and pans, tin plates and cups, coffee pots, utensils, coffee, salt, sugar, flour, dried beans, potatoes, chewing tobacco, smoking tobacco and papers, cigars, matches, blankets, ropes, shovels, pegs, hammers, saws, a small portable table, extra ammunition besides what each Ranger carried on his belt and in his saddle bags, and grain for the horses and mules. The Major had said prepare and they did. Besides all that, each Ranger had his chaps, gun belt with or without a holster, pistol, rifle, one or two knives, some had an extra pistol, one or two canteens, large hat, kerchief to protect the neck from the sun, a rain slicker, soap and a towel, extra shirts and pants, vest, extra socks, and long underwear.

At a little past ten o'clock that morning they rode out of Austin together, one company behind another. They were an impressive sight to behold. Many of the citizens of Austin stopped and watched them ride by. It was the first thing they had seen looking like a parade since the beginning of the war. But there was no cheering this time, for the people knew where they were going and what they were doing. They also knew maybe some of them would not come back. They did not think that at the beginning of the war, but the war had taught them that. And Company F had taught them that.

A mile out of town and the three companies split, with Company B turning to the east, Company D turning to the west, and Company E going straight south. The two outward bound companies traveled to the south-east and south-west, not due east or west. In a few miles they knew they would be separated by about ten miles.

After a while Company D turned more south-ward, with Captain Springtown estimating they were as far out as they were supposed to be. Then he sent out riders.

"Ned take the point, Wilford to the east, and Toombs go to the west. It's time you got your feet wet, but keep your powder dry."

Sullivan gave a half salute and a half smile to the Captain and headed off on his own. After a few minutes it dawned on him that he really was on his own, alone now for the first time. Here he was in a strange land with no one there to help him. What if in looking for signs of Comanches he actually found them instead of just signs of them. What then? He would only fight them if they were right on him and he had no choice. What he would try to do was turn and run, get back to the company, fire in the air, try to get help.

He looked at the ground for tracks and at trees and scrubs and bushes to see if there were any broken limbs, anything out of place. But he saw nothing. It looked to him like no human being had ever been there or anywhere near there, wherever he was.

The long hot hours seemed to drag by. The dust was all over him now, in his nose and ears and mouth. He drank water from time to time, but it tasted like a muddy river. He was wet with sweat, but that was good for when the wind blew even a little it had a cooling effect coming through his wet shirt.

He came to a creek bed, but the water was almost dried up. Just a trickle came down it, but it was enough for his horse to drink. He got down, held the reins, and let the horse drink all he wanted. Then he saw something a few yards to his right. He led the horse over to what had been a camp fire. He knelt down and felt of the ashes. They were cold, must have been several days since there was a fire there from the looks of what he saw. He walked toward the creek bed again and saw hoof prints. These were shod horses, white men's horses. No Indians had been there.

He breathed a sigh of relief. Good, he thought, none of what he was looking for, Indian sign.

He looked around some more and saw they had been a messy group of white men. He found some bones of something they had eaten, maybe a deer. There was a broken knife blade in one place, some spent shell casings in another place, and then he saw something that gave him a jolt. He reached down and picked it up. It looked like a small piece of human skin, maybe a couple of inches square, with long black hair attached to it. It had dried in the sun, but still, there was no mistaking what this was.

"Scalp hunters."

That would explain the shell casings and maybe the broken knife. Better look around some more he thought. He tied his horse to the limb of a small tree, and began walking in a large circle. Fifty yards out from the creek bed he came to a clump of trees. He recognized it immediately. There was nothing else like in God's good world. He had become so familiar with it in the war. He thought he was away from all that, but here it was in Texas. He had caught up with it or it had caught up with him. It was the smell of death. He had smelled it with the dead Rangers, but not back at the river with all those dead Indians. They didn't have time to stink before they left them.

He found the Indian in a small clearing among the trees. He had been shot several times it appeared, though with his body now swollen up and black it was hard to tell. He could see he had been scalped for sure.

What should he do now? Should he bury him? No, you don't bury Indians. You leave them just like they would leave you, leave him for the coyotes and the pigs and whatever else eats dead Indians. It did not look like they had found him yet, but smelling like that they would real soon.

Sullivan walked back to his horse, put the small piece of scalp in his saddle bag, mounted up, went across the creek bed, and continued further south.

The sun was beginning its slow descent in the western sky. He turned eastward, hoping to soon catch up to the company.

After a while he came to a set of tracks, many of them. He knew it was Company D. He followed the tracks for several miles and began seeing the smoke from their fires.

He was the last of the outriders to reach the camp. He tied his horse with the others, took off his saddle and carried it over to where the other Rangers had chosen to bed down. He took the piece of scalp out of his saddle bag and walked over to the Captain.

"Find any sign, Sullivan?"

He held out his hand and said, "Yes, Sir, but not the kind you would expect."

"So, we are not alone out here, and not the only ones looking for Comanches. How many dead?"

"Just one. He'd been dead a number of days. This piece was all I saw, but that was enough to tell what happened to him. I didn't see anything else anywhere, no tracks, no sign, nothing."

"Wonder what he was doing by himself? They usually stay together pretty much to guard against just this kind of thing happening to them."

"I found some animal bones, maybe a deer, maybe a doe, hard to tell since they were scattered all around. Maybe he killed the deer for those he was with, and before he got back to them the whites saw him. Looked like they ate his deer."

"Entirely possible. Well, get some supper. It's edible."

Sullivan filled his plate with the food, beans and dried beef, and walked over and sat down near Crawford.

"Find any Indians, Sullivan?"

"Just one."

"What happened?"

"Nothin'. Somebody else found him first. Scalp hunters."

15

Two days later the Rangers of Company D arrived in San Antonio. They found the other two companies were already there. They put their horses in a livery stable, and checked into a hotel for the night. After sleeping on the ground, a bed would be nice.

Sullivan had never been to San Antonio, though he felt like he had. He had been looking forward to seeing the Alamo. He had heard and read about the famous battle there and the beginning of Texas. Now he would get to see the place. But the first order of business was a good meal.

He, Ned Crawford, Blacky White, and G. W. Smith found a cantina close to the hotel. They went inside and sat down at a table.

It was crowded with other Rangers and also local people. The late afternoon rays from the sun came through a window on the left side of the room. Other than that, it was a dimly lit place and would be even worse when the sun went down. The air was filled with the aroma of cigar smoke, beer, whiskey, highly seasoned food, and sweat.

A white woman stood by the piano and was attempting to sing, though not having much luck. Now and then the piano player looked up at her and smiled. She was not all that bad, just not very good. And she was mostly drowned out by all the loud talk and laughter.

Mexican women walked around among the tables. They talked to the men, sometime asking if they needed more food or drink. At other times they flirted with them. Now and then a man and a woman walked up the stairs. A man staggered to the bar, propped himself on it, and asked for a bottle. Before the bartender could hand it to him the man fell in the floor. No one seemed to mind or came to his aid. He just lay there.

A Mexican woman came up to Crawford and his friends and spoke first.

"What would you like to eat this evening?"

"Steaks all around," answered Ned Crawford. "And bring us some beer and some bread."

"Si, Senior."

"You been here before?" Sullivan asked as the young lady walked away.

"A number of times. We always try to stay here in town and eat right here when we are coming through this area. It's the last good meal from here on south."

As Sullivan looked around, he said to the other three, "I notice a lot of Mexicans here."

Blacky White replied, "These are mostly Texicans. Some Mexicans here, but these other Spanish speakers are all from right here. They speak English too. They live around here, some in town, some on ranches in the area."

Before anyone else could speak a man walked up to them. He wore the wide-brimmed sombrero, had a fancy black belt with silver inlaid, an expensive looking vest, and long spurs on his boots that dragged behind his steps and clanked on the floor. He had a Navy Colt stuffed down under his belt. He had a silver mustache and silver hair at his temples.

"May I join you gentlemen for a moment?"

"Sure," replied Crawford, "pull up a chair."

"Gracias."

The man reached for a chair at a nearby table, dragged it over and sat down.

"My name is Juan Rafael Cortez. I take you gentlemen are Rangers?"

"We are," Crawford replied. "I'm Ned Crawford. That's Sullivan, White, and Smith," he said as the pointed to each of them.

They talked for a few minutes about San Antonio, the hot weather, Toombs Sullivan being new to Texas and to the Rangers, and then Cortez zeroed his attention in on Crawford.

"You are here for a reason, no?"

"Here for a reason, yes."

"Perhaps you are looking for the Comanche?"

"We are."

"I would like for you to catch them. I have a ranch west of here. Many cattle and horses, but the number goes up and down, you see. The Comanche help themselves to what I have from time to time. Is that how you say it?"

"Yes. It means often. Sort of often. Or now and then."

"From time to time they raid my place and take away my cattle and horses. Maybe both at the same time, or maybe just one and not the other."

"There's a lot of that goin' on."

"I know you cannot stop all of them. But maybe you could kill the head of the snake and that would help."

"You speaking of one particular Indian?"

"Particular?"

"One Indian, one Comanche leader."

Two women brought their meals and put them down on the table. They nodded, bowed slightly, and backed away. Two other women delivered the beer and bread, nodded, bowed, and backed away.

"Would you join us?" asked Crawford.

"I have already eaten. Please, please."

"Well excuse us. We haven't eaten all day. Go ahead."

"The head of the snake is a Comanche named Nacona Pledger."

"Sounds like the last name is white," G. W. Smith said as he stabbed his steak with a knife.

"Si. His mother is a white. She was captured as a young girl. When of age she became the wife of a chief and the mother of a son she named Nacona. That name means one who wanders. All the Comanches wander, so a good name for him. Her name is Caroline Pledger."

"Tell us more," Crawford said with a large piece of steak bulging out the side of his face as he chewed, a knife in his right hand and a fork in his left, his arms propped on the table.

"He has become the fiercest war chief of the Comanche. He is the one you are looking for, I think. If you are looking for the one who killed all the Rangers to the south of here."

"Oh, really?" Crawford said as he put down his knife and fork.

"Si. He has several bands who see him as their leader. There may be two, three hundred, four or more whenever they all come together."

"And just where would we find this one who wanders?"

"He is everywhere. He is like the wind. He is the eagle who flies in the day and the owl who attacks in the night. He has hundreds with him for a raid and the next day he may be one man alone. No one among us has ever seen him. Those who see him never tell. They die as soon as they see him. When they see him it is too late."

"Sounds like a dangerous man."

"Most dangerous. The scourge of this land. I speak not just for myself, but for others as well. Can you help us?"

"That's why we are here, Sir, though we did not know his name or that there was one Indian who was the leader of all this. I'll tell our Captain all about him. I'm sure he'll want to go after him."

"Gracias, gracias, Senior. And as you say in English, thank you . . . . very . . . . much."

With that Juan Rafael Lopez stood up, placed the chair back where it had been, and walked away.

"Well, well," Smith said, with his bushy eyebrows raised up, "that shore is interestin'."

"Shore is. Yep," White added.

Sullivan's mouth was full of steak. He simply nodded his head.

Thirty minutes later they had finished their meal, and Crawford said, "Sullivan wants to see the Alamo, but we better not go over there at night. It's an army depot now, Sullivan, and we might get shot if we go snooping around."

Sullivan said, "Sure, we don't want to get shot, not by our own, and not tonight."

"What we better do is go find the Captain, and tell him what we just learned about one who wanders."

They walked back up the street, crossed it, and went in the hotel. They found Captain Springtown sitting in a stuffed chair, reading a newspaper. He had changed his clothes and wiped the dust off his boots. Smoke drifted up from behind the paper. They could see the top of his head and knew it was him.

Crawford said to him, "Captain, we got somethin' to tell ya."

16

"Yep, I heard that name before, that one that wanders, Nacona," Jedidiah Trumbull said.

The other two Captains were finishing up their breakfast and coffee.

"Just what did ya hear?" Jacob Long asked.

Trumbull looked down in his coffee cup, swirled it around some, and replied, "Not much. Just the name. He's a mystery ghost of sorts. He's just out there."

"All Comanches wander," Oliver Springtown said.

"Yeah," Trumbull replied, "but this one's got a special wander. All I heard one time was that he hits hard and is gone."

"You never mentioned him before."

"No, Oliver, you don't talk about somethin' you know nothin' about."

"It never occurred to you all this latest meanness might be him?"

"Nope, not at all. Like I say, he's a mystery. Maybe he's real, maybe not. Maybe he's just a ghost and the Comanch follow what they think they see and do what they think he would do. I don't know. I ain't Comanch."

Jacob Long rolled himself a cigarette, licked it together, struck a match off his leg, lit it up, and said, "If you wus Comanch I'd take yore scalp right now."

After a brief pause, Trumbull said, "What do we do with this? Still stay split until we find somethin'?"

"I think that's the best idea right now," Springtown answered.

Jacob Long looked at them both, first one and then the other and said "Well, all right then. Let's get gone as soon as we can."

They put their money on the table, pushed their chairs back, and got up and left.

They found their men walking on the wooden sidewalk, sitting in chairs in front of the hotel, some sitting in the lobby waiting for a chance to look at a newspaper, and some standing around in groups.

They called them all together. Springtown spoke for the three Captains.

"All right, Men, we pullin' out'a here soon as we can. We go on south like we came down here, separated. We got an idea that there's a Comanche named Nacona Pledger, a half white, who's the leader of several groups when they get together. He is big medicine for them. He may be the one who wiped out our men earlier. We'll find him, and we'll deal with him in the proper way when we do. So be alert. Keep a sharp eye. Be ready to fight at the drop of a hat. Questions? Captain Long and Company B on the left, with me and D in the middle, and Captain Trumbull and E on the right. Let's get."

The Rangers went up to their rooms to get their personal items. Then they headed over to the livery stable.

As they walked along Crawford said to Sullivan, "I don't like it."

"What would that be?"

"An Indian that is and ain't. He's here, but maybe not. He's a big chief, but he's a mystery ghost who may or may not be real, and may or may not be about to kill ya, but you won't know nothin' till ya wake up dead."

"The way you put it I don't like it either. You think maybe this is just all talk? Maybe he's not out there, but the stories grew up just to scare people."

"It's working. I'm scared. I'm people, and I like livin', and I don't want no ghost comin' after me in the night."

"I'll keep an eye out and protect ya."

"If he don't get you first."

When they got to the stable Crawford and Sullivan put their saddles on their horses, and then they put their saddle bags on them. They checked to make sure the saddles were fastened tight enough. They put their rifles in the scabbards. Sullivan pulled his pistol from under his belt and checked to make sure it was loaded.

They walked back outside as they waited for all the others to be ready to go.

"I been thinking," Sullivan said.

"I don't know if that's good or not. Could lead to trouble. What ya been thinking?"

"There's forty-five of us."

"Yep. That'd be right."

"What if we run into two, three, four hundred Indians?"

"So?"

"That's what I said. So, what then?"

"So, we fight. We are well equipped. Some of them have rifles like ours, some not. Some only got bows and arrows or spears. I think we can handle ourselves all right. I ain't afraid of two hundred Indians. Are you?"

"Well, no, I wouldn't say afraid."

"Except for that mystery ghost. I'm afraid of that. I don't like ghosts."

17

The dust rose up and filled up Toombs Sullivan's nose and mouth and ears. He tried to spit, but nothing came out of his mouth except a little dust and a funny sound. After an hour he was soaking wet. He could see the heat rising far out in front of them, and wondered how anything could live in such a place. Now and then he saw the skull of a cow and other bones lying around, of what he could not tell. It did not matter to him.

This is such a hard country he thought. Why all the fuss and fight to hold onto it by the Spanish and the Indians and now the Texans? And yes, the Texicans. They all wanted it and were willing to fight and kill and claw and scrape and die for it. And once you have won it, what do you have?

"What you thinking about so hard there?" asked Ned Crawford.

"Why in the name of God and Heaven and the Holy Bible does anybody want this god-forsaken country?"

"To keep the other fella from having it."

"Is that all?"

"It ain't quite that simple. But that's a big part of it. Another part is that it's so big and wide and spread out here that a man can lose himself or find himself, whichever it is he's wantin'. It has everythin' you could possibly want, fertile farm land, grazin' for cattle, rivers and springs and lakes, trees and lumber, and just the open country where a man can make up a dream and then make that dream come true if he's a mind to do it. You can dream big in Texas. But in all honesty, it has its other side as well. You can have somethin' here and lose it real quick. You can be killed by Indian, crook, robber, thief, Mexican, snake, mountain lion, wild horse, wild cow, and wild women."

"So, it's like every place else?"

"Yep, but bigger and better."

"And hotter."

"That too, and I forgot to mention you can freeze your rear off here as well."

"Gets cold, eh?"

"Yep. That north wind comes down from Canada in the winter, down across the plains, and there ain't a darn thing to stop it. I seen cows froze to death. I seen an Indian froze to his horse and the horse was froze and they wus in mid-air jumping across a creek, just kinda hanging there in the freezin' air. Apache I think he might have been."

"The Indian or the horse? Apache?"

"Both. I knowed it weren't no Comanche. He would've turned tail and run, beat the wind to Mexico."

"What if we don't find this Nacona Pledger?"

"Oh, you ain't got to worry about that none. When he hears we out here lookin' for him, then he'll find us. And he'll hear about it, you can bet on it."

"How?"

"We'll run into some peaceful Indians or Mexicans or people who know Comancheros. They all have contacts with each other and with the Comanches. That's cause they trade with each other and buy stuff and they talk, pass along news about who is here and who ain't. Nacona already knows about them we killed at the river, and he knows since we did not find him, we would be back again. He knows we know he's the one who killed the Rangers, when actually we did not even know of him until the other day. Them at the river was with him then, so we done away with some of his people. That shorely raised up his bristles. And he has to pay a debt now because of that."

"So, are we hunting him or is he hunting us?"

"Yep. We'll find one another by and by. Sooner or later we gonna make contact with them and him."

"That what happened to Company F?"

"Yeah, I would say so. They probably just accidentally ran up on them, and they didn't know what they wus up agin."

"How long you been doing this?"

"Oh, since a few year before the war. I tried ranchin' like my folk. But when they wus dead and gone, my heart weren't in it no more. I seen a lot of bad stuff and wrong stuff and killin' and all. So, I joined the Rangers and been glad I did ever since. Course the war interfered with that somewhat, being as I wasn't here, like all the rest of us. But I came home to it, and I was determined to stay with it until this land calms down."

"How long you think that'll be?"

"I ain't seen no sign that it'll be any time soon."

18

That afternoon a rider from Company E came rushing toward Springtown and Company D. It was Ranger Dexter Stackhouse. He pulled up in front of Springtown.

"The Cap'n sent me to tell ya to come along quick and get Company B. We found lots of sign along the Hondo River, t'other side and this'un. Might be all them Comanch and the ghost."

"Tell him we're on the way. Ned! Go get Company B, and no ya can't take Sullivan with ya!"

Nearly an hour later the three companies were together looking at tracks by the river, both in the dry dirt and also along the wet mud at the very edge. These showed there had been many un-shod horses there.

"What ya make of it?" Captain Springtown asked Sergeant Pete Blankenship.

"Hard to tell how many, but I would say a lot, maybe fifty or a hundred even."

"That's what I was thinking. Well," Springtown called out to the other two Captains, "let's just follow these along and see where they go."

"We'll take the other side while it's still shallow here," Captain Turnbull replied.

He and Company E crossed the river and proceeded along the other shore, searching as they went.

"They really call this Hondo Creek," Ned Crawford explained to Toombs Sullivan. "It ain't deep here at all, as you could see when they went, but on down it gets deep. Fact is the word Hondo means deep. It's Spanish. It runs into the Frio River."

They followed the tracks along the river for about five miles. Then they stopped to water the horses and get down and stretch and yawn and smoke.

Ned Crawford said to Sullivan, "Back in forty-two there was a big fight here with the Mexicans. It's called the Battle of Arroyo Hondo. They got their butts kicked here and went running on down to Mexico. It took place a ways on down."

"Ned! Ride on ahead and see what's down there," shouted Captain Springtown.

"Sure, Cap'n. See ya later."

"Five more minutes," Springtown said to all of them. "If ya got to do it, do it now!"

Several of the men stood along the river's edge as Wilford Boyd said to Sullivan, "There ain't nothin' like peein' in the river."

Toombs Sullivan joined in.

Another ten miles and they came upon Ned Crawford as he helped a man load two bodies on a pack horse. They were at the edge of a thick growth of Mesquite trees along both sides of the river.

Ned walked over to Springtown and said, "I didn't want to leave this man by hisself, Cap'n and come get ya. These is two of his sons. They was out down here gathering up their cows that wandered off away from their place back over yonder a few miles. One of 'em is nineteen, t'other about sixteen he said. They's a third one that's twelve, but he ain't nowhere around. He thinks the Comanches took him to raise maybe. They took the cattle with them. They's a lot of their horse tracks and the tracks of the cows all mixed together from here on down. There ain't no doubt what happened. The Indians just wandered upon these three, and decided they wanted the cattle. The boys had camped here a night or two. The ashes from their fire are right over there. And Cap'n, what they did to these two boys is ungodly. They sliced them and diced them and cut off everthin' about them. I hate for a man to see that done to his sons."

"What's his name?"

"William Peele."

"Mister Peele," Springtown said as he approached the distraught man, "I'm mighty sorry this happened. We're chasing these Indians. We'll find them and do some justice, and I hope we find your youngest doing all right and we can bring him home to ya."

William Peele was a tall, thin, gaunt looking man who wore a big black hat. He had a dark complexion and several days of black beard growth on his face. His eyes were red. He had tracks down his dusty face where the tears had run. He had a look on his face that was a mixture of sorrow, shock, disbelief, and terror.

"Thank you, Sir . . . . Please bring my boy home. He's all we got left now."

"We'll do our best. I can send one of our men with you to help get these two home."

"No, Captain. Some things a man got to do by himself, on his own. This is one of them. The wife'll be waiting on us. I got to deliver them myself."

"I understand. Name of your son?"

"Thomas. These two are . . . . were Willie and Herman."

William Peele wiped his face and took a deep breath.

"I shouldn't have sent them out here. Should have come myself, alone. But they been doing this for years. Yore cattle wander off down here, and ya have to go get them back. If ya don't the Mexicans'll take them . . . . or the Indians. And they'll take ya life, they will. They did."

"We'll do our best to find Thomas."

Springtown shook the man's hand and walked away. He went over to Captain Jacob Long.

"How far ahead ya think?"

"From the look of these tracks, I'd say a day. Maybe this happened last night or late yesterday. Your man, Ned, that got here said to me them boys been dead a while, what's left of 'em, startin' to swell up and all."

"It's gettin' late. When he gets gone maybe we better set up camp here for the night."

A few minutes later William Peele disappeared over a little hill, trailing his pack horse behind him.

Sullivan looked at Ned Crawford, "Why'd he know to bring the horse?"

"Out here some things ya just know."

The Rangers began making camp by the river. They unloaded their mules, put the tables in place, started fires, began preparing supper, and posted guards. But the first order of business was letting the horses drink, and then getting in the water themselves, not only to bathe, but also to cool off.

They sat around eating and smoking, and engaging in one of their favorite things, talking about the war. They had many theories about how things went, how they should have gone, what should have been done, and how they should have won.

Sullivan got up and walked along the river. He did not like these kinds of conversations, other than saying yes he was there, and yes he fought, and yes he went home early. Thinking and talking about the war always led him to think about coming home after the war and what he found when he got there. It was the end of everything. It was too painful to keep going over all that again and again.

So, he walked along the river's edge. He looked at the water and the trees and the hills beyond, though they were not much in the way of hills. They were more like little slopes and rises. Texas, that part of Texas, could use a few good hills.

The sun was slowly passing away in the west. A few shadows were beginning to lengthen. He heard the lonely call of a dove, and threw a rock in the river.

19

That night the three Captains sat near a fire and pondered the next day. Oliver Springtown spoke first.

"I think we may need to stay together now that we have their trail. Pushing those cattle, even though they are only a few, will slow them down. We may catch up with them real quick. That means we need all our guns together."

"I agree," Jedidiah Trumbull replied. "We don't need to take no chances now."

"So how do we approach them?" asked Jacob Long.

Springtown thought for a moment as he reached over and took a small burning stick from the fire, lit a long, thin cigar he held between his teeth, threw the stick back in the fire, inhaled the smoke deeply, and blew it out slowly. With the cigar in his right hand, he rubbed his face on both sides with his left hand. Then he looked at each of the other two men.

"How about we stampede them? I'll send my best rider out ahead, Ned Crawford, and let him find them. Then we'll come up slow, quiet, easy like until we get as close as we can. Then we cut dirt and charge them like General Forrest after Yankees."

"What about the boy?" Trumbull asked.

"We'll have to take a chance. If they get wind of us behind them, they'll do whatever they would if we pounce on them quickly, so what's the difference?"

Long nodded his head, and said, "His chances may be better if we surprise them anyway."

"You think the mystery ghost, Nacona Pledger, is in this group?" Trumbull asked.

Springtown raised his eyebrows, scratched the left side of his head, and said, "Who knows? If he is and suddenly disappears, we'll know he really is a mystery ghost. I can only say I hope he is and we can kill him outright."

Sullivan came back from his walk and he, Crawford, and G. W. Smith were sitting close enough to hear what was being said by the Captains.

"They're talking about you," Sullivan said to Crawford. "Sounds like you get to go out front again."

"Sometime it don't pay to do a good job. You get known for it, and then yore name gets called for the worst kind of things."

Then G. W. Smith said, "I remember one time when me and another old boy was sent out to find some Yankees who was supposed to be camped near us. Hell, we went right past them and didn't even see'em. Then we doubled back, and before we knew it, we was standing right in the middle of them almost. Then the shootin' started as our company caught up with them, and we killed ten or fifteen and took about thirty captive. We was lucky we dint get shot by our own men."

"If that happens tomorrow, Crawford won't look like an Indian so he won't get shot, at least not by us," Sullivan said as he and Smith laughed. Crawford did not see any humor in that.

"Ned! You've heard what we said over here?" Springtown called out.

"Yes, Sir. I'll be on it first thing."

"You come back from time to time and give us a report. I want to know everything about what they do, where they stop, what happens, how far out you think they are, and most important, when you finally see them and how far ahead of us they are at that time and place."

"I will, Captain."

"Leave early."

"Yes, Sir."

"I mean real early."

"Yes, Sir."

"And report often."

"Yes, Sir. Anything else?"

"Yeah, shut-up and get some sleep."

G. W. Smith's story about the war had triggered something in Sullivan again. As Smith and Crawford quietly went back to their conversation, Sullivan got up and walked off again. He went over to check on his horse. Finding him all right, he returned to his friends. Then Springtown called to him.

"Sullivan, take the guard. I'll relieve ya in a couple of hours."

"Sure, Captain."

He walked out to where Willard Boyd was standing guard, and said to him, "I'm yore relief. Get some sleep."

"Thanks. Take charge."

Sullivan looked out into the black night. Anyone standing guard would not have a chance if some Indians were out there crawling toward him, he thought. He might as well just go stand by the fire and wait on them there. But he knew he was over-reacting, thinking too much. The Indians were not out there. But he was just as well off standing guard as he would be trying to sleep. Sleeping was not easy for him on some of those nights. Too much had happened, and too many thoughts ran through his mind.

20

Before dawn Ned Crawford rode out in search of the Comanche band. He was nervous about it, fearing he would catch up with them before he realized how close he had gotten. He could not help but think about G. W. Smith's story of running up on and past those Yankees. He would just have to be very alert. He had done things like this before many times.

.... Toombs Sullivan felt the cool breeze of a late September day blow lightly across his face. He saw it in the limbs of the trees and as it swayed the tall grass. He saw her coming toward him, all smiles and a loving gentleness that had always warmed his heart. He had always loved her, and had never gotten her out of his mind even in the thick of battle. And he knew it was dangerous to think about her in such situations. But here she was again running toward him. Her hair slightly blowing in the breeze like the tall grass. She reached out arms to hold him and then . . . .

Suddenly he and the other Rangers were awakened by the Captains just as the first light came up over the hills to the east. The Captains had been up a while, had started the fires and put on the coffee pots.

Sullivan stood up, stretched, yawned, and looked around. He ran his right hand through his hair and scratched his head. He yawned again as he smelled the coffee, and looked to find the source of that pleasing aroma. He walked over to the small portable table where the tin cups were stacked, picked one up, and asked "Ready?"

"Help yourself," Springtown replied.

"Hot," he said as he tasted the coffee.

"Sleep good?"

"As well as a man can out here on the ground."

"It could be a rough day. Be alert always."

"If I drink enough of this boilin' stump water I will be I guess."

An hour later all the men had eaten, dressed, saddled their horses, loaded their gear, and got the mules loaded. They were ready to pull out.

G. W. Smith said to Sullivan, "Ya ready for this?"

"Sure, I been ready. Nothing to it. Easy as pie. Let me at'em."

"You truthin' me or what?"

"What ya think?"

"I don't know. It's why I asked, of course."

"How ya get ready to kill humans?"

"These people ain't humans. They somethin' else altogether."

"Yeah, I know. I am ready to do it for sure. I know it got to be done. And, yeah, I like it once we get into it."

"Listen up!" Captain Trumbull said. "Now, we got a rider out locatin' the Comanches. He'll let us know when he finds them. A reminder, they have cattle and are likely movin' slow. When we get near, we'll be careful not to alarm them. When we're as close as we can get, we'll go shootin' into the middle of them. Do not dismount. Stay on your horse and you'll do better. If we can surprise them and get into the midst of'em we'll use our pistols. If you have a second one, have it ready. Don't take time to reload your first. If we don't get close then our rifles will be better. You'll know which when the fightin' starts. Questions? All right then, let's be movin' out."

The Rangers mounted up and began heading south with Springtown's Company D in the lead. They were followed by Company B and then Company E, but the two Captains of those Companies rode up front with Springtown. They followed the trail of the Comanche horses and the cattle, and they could also see Crawford's tracks from earlier in the day.

Sullivan was nervous about this encounter, regardless of what he had said to Smith. Shooting Indians from that ridge was one thing, but now they were to ride into them close up. Close enough for pistols was too close for him. He knew this is what they should do, kill as many as they could. They deserved it after what they did to those boys, but it was a savage thing, as savage as the Indians. Was there any difference in the Indians and the Rangers? He was beginning to wonder about that. Still it had to be done to protect other people, to have law and order, to tame that country, and yes, for revenge. Maybe revenge was a sweet thing. It had its own satisfaction. And it came from a perfect hatred, the kind of hatred that allows a man to strike down another and enjoy it, love it, bask in it. He could enjoy that, but every time he admitted that to himself, he felt a twinge of guilt. But the guilt did not last long. He had learned how to subdue it, dismiss it, and get on with whatever he had to do. It had been that way with the Yankees. After every battle he had his own private war inside, a struggle with the guilt of that mad business. Yet, he was always ready for the next time, the next opportunity to spill blue blood over green grass and love it. Revenge was indeed the sweetest reward of all.

In a little more than two hours Ned Crawford came riding back to the column. Sullivan was close enough to the front of the column to hear what he reported.

"Captain, I found where they camped last night. They're not too far ahead of us. With good speed we could catch them by noon. But on beyond where they camped four of their horses split off headed more west, south-west, I reckon. I didn't see no other places where any of the rest of them left the main party."

The three Captains looked at each other, and Springtown spoke first, "If we split off some of our men to go after those four then we weaken ourselves. Our other choice is stay together and hit the main group with all we have. What ya think?"

Captain Trumbull said, "That's what we need to do."

"I agree," Captain Long answered.

"All right. Men, pass the word back that it won't be too long now, a matter of a few hours. And watch out for that Peele boy."

Three hours later the sun was straight up. Crawford had ridden on ahead. The little cloud of dust in the distance revealed he was on his way back. Soon he was slowing down and stopping in front of the Captains.

"There's a little hill 'bout a mile on down. They just takin' a little rest on the other side for a spell. They likely won't see us if we go slow up that hill and don't create no dust storm."

"Lead us to it," Springtown said. "Pass the word. This is it. All quiet and slow."

Sullivan put his hand on his pistol just to assure himself he knew where it was. He took a deep breath and sat up straight in his saddle. The sweat ran down from his temples to below his jaw. He held the horse's reins with his right hand and wiped the sweat from around his mouth with the sleeve of his left arm. Sweet revenge, he thought, and a perfect hatred. This was going to be good, the ultimate good, good in the midst of bad maybe. No matter, it was not for him to make such decisions. He was a Ranger, just a Ranger. He did what he was told, just like everyone else. It was like in the war, the god-awful war. You do what you are told to do. The right and the wrong, the guilt and the innocence, the good and the bad was not up to him. It was up to whoever was in charge. Just hold on, aim as well as ya can from horseback, shoot those you can, protect yourself. He was ready.

21

The column stopped just before the little hill. The three Captains turned around and signaled the men to spread out in a line. Forty-five Texas Rangers pulled out their pistols, held them in their right hands with their reins in their left hands. They walked their horses slowly along as they approached the rise. They stopped just short of it as Ned Crawford dismounted, bent down low and crept up to where he could look over on the other side. Then while staying low, he came back to the Captains and whispered, "They're still there, cooking some of them beefs."

It was clear then the Comanches were there for a day of rest and then the night. That meant they would be relaxed, confidant with no guards out, feeling they were entirely safe. It was the perfect time to hit them.

Crawford hopped back up on his horse as Captain Springtown yelled out, "Let's go!"

Over the hill they rushed, horses charging, dirt flying up, Rangers screaming out like Rebel soldiers, gun-shots blasting the air and shattering the silence, and smoke from the pistols rolling down toward the Indians.

The Comanches began falling to the ground, screaming out as the bullets ripped through them, their blood flying through the air in blotches, their ponies panicking and running away. And they began running after their ponies. Those who could reach then jumped on them and rode off to the south. Others picked up their rifles and spears and bows and arrows and tomahawks and began fighting back, bringing down several Rangers. Some of the Rangers were pulled off their horses and were fighting with the Indians close up, slashing them with their Bowie knives, ramming them as far into their enemy's stomachs and chests and throats as they could.

Sullivan managed to stay on his horse. He emptied his pistol and then pulled out his rifle and used it. When he had emptied it, he began swinging it like a club. Then suddenly a Camanche was on the back of his horse trying to pull him off of it. Fearing a knife in the back, he flipped himself backward causing him and the Indian to go sprawling in the dirt. He pulled out his Bowie knife and held it up as the Indian dove onto him. In an instant he was covered with the blood of the Indian. He rolled him over and pulled his knife out of the Indian's stomach. He jumped up and looked around, and picking up a spear he rammed into the back of an Indian who was about to get the best of Springtown who was lying on the ground. He grabbed another spear and killed an Indian running toward him with a tomahawk held high and back as he was about to swing it. Sullivan then took the tomahawk and waded into a group of Indians fighting several Rangers. He brought down one after another.

Suddenly the battle was over, and a deathly silence fell upon the ground as it had the Rangers and especially the dead Comanches. The Rangers looked around and saw there was not an Indian standing. Then they quickly rushed to take care of their wounded. Several Rangers had gun-shot wounds or wounds from the Indian's other weapons. Then they saw that seven Rangers were dead, shot or dead from spears or their heads split open from the tomahawks.

When the wounded had been cared for, bandaged and patched up, they began looking around at the dead Indians lying everywhere. They had killed forty-one of them, almost one apiece. They estimated another eighty or ninety had managed to escape. As they looked closer, they saw the tracks of those who had escaped during the fight, but there was an older set of tracks heading off to the south-west. They could not tell how many had left earlier, perhaps even the night before. But it looked like a large number. At first, they were sorry so many had gotten away earlier, but as they stood around, they realized they were lucky they did not face the whole large group that had been together.

Then the Captains began thinking about what they did not find.

"Don't look like a mystery ghost among all these dead," Trumbull said.

"No cattle. They must have eat them all or were about to," Long said. "And there's no women and children here either."

Then Springtown added, "And no white boy named Peele."

Toombs Sullivan stood over several of the dead Comanches. Then he walked all around and looked at each one of them on the ground. The lifeless forms lay there in silence, no breathing and now no blood coming out of them as their hearts no longer pumped any out. Some had their eyes closed as though they were merely sleeping, while others were staring off at the sky, the trees, each other. They lay in odd positions with their black hair flowing over their faces or pulled behind or under them, arms and legs twisted in various ways. Sullivan had never gotten over the quiet solitude of the dead he first saw early in the war. They made no complaint now, uttered no protest, offered no explanation, made no demands. They simply accepted their fate. But Sullivan felt they were inviting him to join them, to come and go where there was no war and no fighting and no more suffering. He felt the pull of the dead upon him, and secretly he wondered how it might be to enter the calm world of the dead. He longed to join his wife and son, to spend eternity with them, and to find the peace these Indians now enjoyed. His private contemplation was interrupted by the voice of Captain Springtown.

"Awright, let's get some shovels and bury our dead. Put them in a line ov'there under that tree. Some of ya see if you can make some crosses."

"Captain," Sullivan said, "I noticed something here."

"What is it?"

"Look over here. This one has a Ranger badge, and he's wearing a vest that belonged to somebody."

"So, he was with them, and I guess these were all the ones who did it."

"And there are two more over there with badges."

"I'm glad we got'em."

"It's called sweet revenge, Captain, and a perfect hatred."

Springtown looked at Sullivan for a moment, and had a strange and quizzical look on his face. Then he said, "I guess I never heard it put that way before, but yes, that's good, that's good."

It made Springtown wonder about Toombs Sullivan. There was something going on inside of his head, and it might not be all that good. He wondered if Sullivan might be on the edge of something that was not healthy. But there was no time to wonder about such things. They had Indians to catch and kill, with yes, a perfect hatred.

Then the three Captains with a couple of the men began slicing great slabs of meat off the beef that was cooked. They wrapped them up, and made ready to pursue the Indians.

When the dead Rangers were in the ground Captain Springtown took his Bible out and read from it. Then Captain Trumbull said a few words about the men. Captain Long said a short prayer.

Gone were G. W. Smith and Blackie White from Company D, Slim Simmons, Ted Granger, and Reggie Cook from Company B, Arnold Coldtree and George Craig from Company E. They died in the line of duty and in the faith. Their deeds would now go before them as they were gathered unto their fathers.

Over an hour after the battle had begun the Rangers mounted up and headed south after the Comanches who now would not be slowed by the cattle they no longer possessed.

None of the wounded men had anything that was serious enough to slow them. They could ride and were ready for another fight, wanting to avenge their dead brothers.

22

L ate in the afternoon it became apparent the Rangers would not catch up with the Comanches that day. They stopped along the Frio River and set up camp for the night. The horses needed rest as well as the wounded men. Their hour of administering more judgment would have to wait at least another day.

The first thing they did was to water the horses and mules. Then they took the portable tables from the mules and set them up. Some of the men gathered fire wood, built fires, and put the beef over the fires to heat it and cook it some more. There was no breeze causing the aroma of the cooking meat to lay softly over the low place by the river where they made their camp.

The Captains looked at the wounded men, changed their bandages, and made sure there was no serous bleeding. They posted guards just to protect against the possibility the Comanches might double back on them, for surely they knew they were being pursued. The horses were tied in a line in a small meadow by the river. Their backs were dried of the sweat on them after the long day. Then the men undressed and went in the water.

Toombs Sullivan stood waste deep in the river. He lifted up cupped hands of water and let it flow down over his head and face. He submerged himself and stood back up with all the dust and dirt and grime and blood now washed away. But could he ever be clean again after all he had been through and all he had done? He had gotten some sweet revenge and had acted upon and let out that perfect hatred he possessed or which possessed him, but he wondered if he would ever be clean again.

Later in the evening the Rangers sat around the fires or on stumps or large boulders. They ate the meat and canned beans they had brought with them. They drank coffee that tasted like the river. They talked about the battle that day, the Indians they had killed and their brothers who had been taken away from them. Ned Crawford looked over at Sullivan.

"You som'ers else again?"

"Nope, I'm right here. I just look like a crazy man."

"You ain't confused about killin' these Indian devils, are you?"

"No. I ain't. I killed my share."

"I noticed. I got a glimpse of ya choppin' away with that tomahawk. You ain't bad with it."

"Just doin' what comes natural, I guess."

"Seemed to be."

"But I been wonderin'. What good is all this doin'? I know why we're after them. I agree it is the thing to do after all they done. I want to kill all of them. I even got a taste of blood in my mouth now and I like it. I like killin' them. But ain't there no end to it? Even if we could kill all these we're after, where's the end? There would just be more and more comin'. And the killin' will never stop."

"Oh, it'll stop all right. We'll kill the last one and his son and that'll be the end of 'em. Then peace will come to this land. There won't be no more killin' of the whites."

Captain Springtown walked over to the two men and said, "Well, Sullivan that's the second time you saved my life. I was about to get it from that Comanch, but you got there with just the right thing at just the right time."

"Just doin' my job, Captain. That's what I get paid to do."

"I am indebted to ya."

"Maybe tomorrow, or whatever day it is, you'll have a chance to return the favor."

"I will indeed."

With that Springtown walked away. As he did Crawford said, "Georgia Boy, you come in right handy."

"I aim to please."

They continued to talk for a while, until the sun was completely gone, and then later the moon rose in the sky, and they saw all the stars in the heavens . . . .

A feeling of peace came over Sullivan as he stood in the field with the new spring sun warming him. But it was nothing like the warmth of his love for Constance as he saw her walking gracefully toward him. The light blue dress she wore fit close around her neck and the sleeves came down to her wrists. She held her ankle-length skirt up slightly as she walked through the grass that was nearly knee high and was blown softly by the breeze. And her hair was blown softly. She walked up to him and put her arms around him. He embraced her and held her close. He could smell the lilac perfume she often placed under her chin and along her neck. He buried his face in her long flowing hair on the right side of her neck. Holding her was the closest thing to heaven he had ever known. Suddenly their son rushed up to them and hugged both their legs. What more could a man want? There was nothing better than this. He placed his left hand on the boy's head. His son looked up at him and smiled. And then . . . .

"Wake up, fool. Let's go kill some Indians."

"What?"

Ned Crawford laughed at Sullivan and said, "Where you been?"

"Oh. Right here."

"Well, we're leaving. It's a good day for killin'. Better get ready."

"I am ready," Sullivan said as he took in his hand the cup of coffee Ned held out to him, and then as he drank it, he went to get his horse.

They mounted up as Sullivan finished the coffee and placed the cup on his saddle bag.

"This might be the day when we finish them off," Crawford called out.

"Right. This could be the day."

But Sullivan wondered if maybe the Indians might not finish them, since they knew they were being pursued. A wounded animal will turn and fight even more viciously than before.

23

On the Rangers rode to the south-west, with Ned Crawford out front by several miles. They had entered the brush country, a no-man's land only the Comanches liked. They knew they would find them that day, and that would be the final judgment day for them. But as they moved further toward them the trail they followed seemed to disappear. Groups of them peeled off on their own away from the main body. The Rangers resisted the temptation to follow these smaller groups. It was a pattern they had seen before. A large group made up of several smaller bands went on a raid, and then after the raid they spilt up. Finally, they were following a small band of maybe thirty or forty Indians.

At mid-morning Ned Crawford came galloping back to the column.

"I found them. They're dead ahead. They must'av thought we'd give up and not come after them. The Nueces River is further on down. Can't be far away. If we can hit them before they get to the river, we got a better chance."

"How far?"

"About a mile or so."

Trumbull called out, "All right, Men, they're not far away! Get ready!"

The Rangers rode on quickly now, pistols drawn, ready for the battle. Soon they saw the Comanches ahead of them. They sped up even more and went charging into them. They had caught them unprepared to fight. The Rangers began firing at them, killing one after another. The Comanches fell from their ponies or by their fires. Some of them turned and charged at the Rangers with their spears at the ready, but they were struck down. Others began shooting arrows, and those who had rifles began firing, but it was too late. It was another brutal battle with guns and knives and spears and tomahawks. Some of the Indians fell wounded off their ponies and managed to stand back up again but were struck down instantly. The Rangers killed all of the Comanche men in a few short minutes. Then they realized what had happened.

The Comanches had met up with their women and children and old men who had been camped and waiting nearby for them. They were huddled in a group off to one side from where the fighting had been. There were over fifty of them standing there in a state of shock. They had just seen husbands and sons and fathers struck down before them. The women began crying out and rushing toward their dead.

Then the Rangers saw them. There was a white woman dressed like an Indian, a white girl, and a white boy, both of them appearing to be about the age of twelve.

The Rangers got off their horses and walked among the dead, making sure they would not be able to rise up and attack them. They did not shoot any of them again for there was no need.

The three Captains approached the whites.

Trumbull said to the boy, "You the Peele boy?"

"Yes, I am. I want to go home."

"You will, Son. And you the Claxton girl?"

"I am," she said as she burst out crying. "My family is all dead."

"I know," Springtown replied. "We'll find you a place. What about you?" he said, turning to the woman. She appeared to be about forty to fifty years old, but she also appeared to be an Indian, a white Indian. Her dark hair had a few steaks of gray. Her skin, though white, was tanned by the sun and showed signs of being rough because of too much exposure to the rays of the sun. She wore a buckskin dress with beads on it and also buckskin boots that reached to her knees. She had a band around her head with many colored beads on it and a matching belt. There were bracelets on both of her wrists.

"My name is Caroline Pledger."

"What?"

"Caroline Pledger."

"Are you . . . ."

"I am. Why have you come here?"

"We've come to stop the killin' of these savages."

"Savages? Who is the savage? I stood here and watched what you did. Why did you not kill us as well?"

"Are you . . . ."

"Yes. I am the mother of Nacona Pledger. You have come here to kill him, but you will never be able to do that. You will never see him. My people and even the Mexicans speak of him as the mystery ghost. When you do see him, it will be too late. You will be dead in the next moment."

"Where is he?"

"Do you think I would tell you? If he were here you would be dead now."

"Well, we've come to set you free. We'll take you back to Austin."

"I have nothing in Austin. These are my people. This is my place."

"You're a white. You belong back there in the white world and not out here livin' like this. Where'd all those other Comanches go that made up that big group doin' all the killin' and stealin'?"

"They have gone to the winds. You will never find them, but they will find you. My son will come in the night out of the shadows and kill you in your sleep. Or maybe he will be in the brightness of the sun so that you stumble into his spear without ever seeing it."

"That may be, but you're goin' with us. We're taking you home."

"I am home. I will not stay wherever you take me."

"Somebody fetch the horses that belonged to Smith, White, and one other for these three! Then ever-body get ready to mount up! We're taking these people home."

Then Springtown turned to Ned Crawford and Toombs Sullivan, and said, "I want you two to take this boy and girl home. I hope the Boutwells will take the girl, she being the closest neighbor and all. She got nobody else. We'll take the Pledger woman on to Austin. You meet us there when you can."

Both men nodded and led their horses to where the two children were as others brought them horses to ride.

Crawford and Sullivan walked closer to the two youngsters. Crawford spoke first.

"You two all right?"

They both nodded their heads.

"They treat you bad or good?"

The Peele boy looked at the girl, and said, "I guess we were treated all right. They didn't harm us in any way. They fed us, and the ones who speak English said we would be taken care of, and would be taken in by families that would see to our raisin'."

Then Sullivan asked, "Did you see an Indian named Nacona Pledger?"

The boy replied, "We never heard the name of any of them."

"Was there one that was in charge, a chief?"

"I don't know."

"He is that white woman's son. Did you see anything that might make you think that?"

"We don't know nothin', Mister. We just want to go home."

"All right. Home it is."

24

The column pulled out, headed back north-east as Crawford and Sullivan took a more northerly route. They watched as the dust from the column slowly disappeared, and realized now they were alone. Now and then they looked back to see if the children were still with them and found they were both good riders.

The next day they arrived at the Boutwell's ranch and were warmly greeted. They made sure they went around the Claxton place so as not to upset the girl.

"Yep, we remember you folk," said Jim Boutwell. Then he exclaimed, "My God! You found the girl! Jesse, the girl!"

Jesse Boutwell came out of the house drying her hands on her apron. She pushed her hair back, and said as she approached the girl, "Oh, Child, bless yore heart. Come to me." Then she helped her down from her horse.

"Get down, Boys, get down," Jim Boutwell said. "Water yore horses and have some yore-self. We'll feed ya."

"Thanks," both Rangers said at the same time.

As they were eating at the table the two children went outside to look around when they had finished. Then Crawford said, "We was thinking that maybe you folk would take the girl. She got nobody else, and we wouldn't know where to take her."

"Of course we will," Jesse Boutwell said. "We've known her all her life. I'm so thankful you found her. We thought we would never see her again, poor thing."

"What about the boy?" Jim Boutwell asked.

"He's the Peele boy. We met his daddy. They live on up a ways. He had two other sons killed by the Comanch. They stole their cows the boys had rounded up, killed them, and took this'un with-em."

"So, you caught up with them and what happened?"

"We administered justice, Texas Ranger justice."

"Well, good. That'll teach'em."

"I'm afraid not," Sullivan said, "The ones that learned a lesson are dead now. The rest got away somewhere and they didn't learn nothin'. They'll be back at it some more."

"We worry about them all the time, but so far we've been lucky."

"Let me fix you another plate," Jesse Boutwell said.

"Oh, not me," Sullivan answered.

"Me neither, Ma'am. We got to get goin'," Crawford said.

"Stay the night. We'll put you up."

"Appreciate it, but we got miles to go, and we need to get the boy back home."

"We understand," she replied.

"Yep," Jim Boutwell agreed.

The two Rangers left with Tommy Peele right behind them. They rode until near dark, then camped. They made a small fire, ate some food the Boutwells had given them, and then drank coffee.

"You think we'll ever get to this Pledger?" Sullivan asked.

"Oh, yeah. One day, one fine day, we'll catch up to him. He can't do what he's doin' and go on forever like that. His luck is gonna run out, and I want to be thar when it does. I want to be the one that does him in. It don't matter to me how or under what circumstance or where it is. Just let me at'im."

The next morning, they were off again, and arrived at the Peele's place about noon.

When they came near the house, the Peeles rushed out to meet them. They both threw their arms around Tommy and hugged him as his mother burst into tears.

The Rangers looked off to the side up a little rise and saw two fresh graves. Then they looked back at the boy's father and saw he had been watching them.

"Well, did ya?"

"We did, Mister Peele," Crawford answered.

"Get down, Men. Have some food. Stay the night."

"Thanks, Sir, but we got to get on toward Austin," Sullivan said.

"I thank ya so much. How can I thank ya? What can we do?"

"Ya don't need to do nothin'. This is our job," Crawford said. "But if ya got a biscuit or two, we'll take them with us," he said as he laughed.

"We got more than two. And you're welcomed to them."

Crawford and Sullivan were then headed off toward Austin, hoping to be there the next day or the following day.

After they had been riding for a couple of hours they stopped for a moment to give the horses a rest.

Sullivan turned around and looked back at where they had been. Then he looked at Crawford.

"I keep having the feeling there's somebody following us."

Crawford looked around and said, "That's because there is. He's been back there most of the day."

"Who you think it is?"

"Who do you think? We got his mama. He prob'ly don't like that very much."

"Maybe we ought to wait on'im, ambush him."

"Won't do no good. Ever-body, including his mama, says we'll never see him. He's the mystery ghost, remember."

"Then, what do we?"

"I'm getting' myself to Austin. You do what you like."

"I'm with ya."

25

Toombs Sullivan stomped his feet on the sidewalk boards to knock the dust and dirt off his boots and pants, and then he walked into the lobby of the hotel. Ned Crawford did the same and came in behind him. They saw Oliver Springtown talking with the clerk at the desk.

"Hello, Boys. I see you made it all right."

"We did," Sullivan replied.

"Get them young'uns home?"

"Yes, Sir. The Boutwells took the girl. And the Peeles were mighty glad to have Tommy back, as you can imagine."

"What about the Pledger woman?" Crawford asked.

"She's upstairs in her room," Springtown answered. "That is one strange woman. She's been with the Indians so long that she is one. I'd heard of it, but I've never seen anything like this in my life. She is a white Indian. She speaks English still as you saw, but sometime she goes into Indian talk and even Spanish and then back to English. It's like she does it without even knowing it. She won't come out of her room. She says she will not stay here. She won't even come out to eat, does not want to be around whites at all. I have to take her food up there so she can eat, but most of it she don't even touch."

"That is strange," Sullivan said. "Why not let her go back if she don't want to be here? I know we thought we were right by her when we brought her out, but, like you say, she ain't white no more. We can't make her want to be white, if she's already Indian."

"I know. I don't know what to do now."

Just then a Mexican woman came out of the kitchen with a tray in her hands.

"Sullivan, go with me and help me get her food to her. Knock on the door and then open it."

"Sure."

The two men walked up the stairs, turned left at the top, and walked down the hall.

"That door down there on the left."

They stopped in front of the door. Sullivan knocked on the door twice, and then he turned around and looked at Springtown.

"She won't answer the door. Open it."

Sullivan opened the door and stepped inside, followed closely by Springtown.

"My God," Sullivan said.

Springtown put the tray down on the small table, and said, "I didn't even know she had a knife. I wasn't about to search her. Guess I should have."

Caroline Pledger lay in a pool of blood, her throat and both wrists cut. The knife was on the floor beside her. It was small with a razor-sharp blade, the kind Indians used for skinning game – and people.

"Must have been down in her boot."

"Yep, maybe so," Springtown answered. "There's nothing to do now but get the undertaker over here to pick her up. Then tomorrow we'll give her a decent burial. I know the Methodist circuit rider here. If he's in town we'll get him to say some words over her."

"English or Indian or Spanish?"

"Yeah. That is the question ain't it."

The next afternoon all the Rangers who had brought Caroline Pledger back to civilization stood in a group around her grave as Reverend Walcott Jenkins read from the Bible, spoke of God's mercy, and said a few prayers. Then three of the Rangers shoveled the dirt over her wooden coffin, the dirt and small rocks hitting the top of it and sounding like rain coming down on a roof. When they finished the three stepped back as they all looked at the pile of dirt where there had been a level place. Two other Rangers took a wooden marker as one held it and the other drove it into the ground with a sledge hammer. On the marker had been carved the words Caroline Pledger.

"Well, that's it," Oliver Springtown said. "Thanks preacher, for doing this."

The preacher had a stern look on his face as he said "God have mercy on her soul." Then he turned and left.

"Let's go eat," Captain Trumbull said.

As they walked away some of the men talked to each other about a variety of things, none of them having to do with what they had just observed or Nacona Pledger or his now deceased mother.

Toombs Sullivan was speaking to no one however. He was deep in thought. He wondered if maybe they had done the wrong thing in bringing Caroline Pledger away from the Indians and back into the white world. He had mentioned that to Springtown earlier, and wondered if they should not have let her go back to where she had spent her entire adult life. In trying to help her they had destroyed her. And it seemed to him the only way they could bring the Indians into the new world was to kill them all. He had been struggling with that all along, but this just served to intensify his thoughts. He was a Texas Ranger. He was sworn to protect white people and uphold the law. That meant going after the Comanches and killing them because they were in a war with them, and there was no way to make peace. He even had to admit to himself that he enjoyed killing them. As soon as they approached the Indians that hatred he had came alive like striking a match to a pile of grass. It burned until it went out with the last Comanche dead. But there were times like this when he was away from the killing and he could think clearly. In those times he wondered what had brought him from being a farmer in Georgia to this, to killing for a living. He wondered what his parents and his wife and son would think about that.

Ned Crawford walked up behind Sullivan and said, "You fixin' the world?"

"Nope. I'm wonderin' what they fixin' for supper. Whatever it is I want some."

"Me too. A lot. Let's stop by the saloon and have a drink or two."

"Sure. But don't mix it up and have a lot to drink and a bite or two at supper."

"That sounds like a good idea. Would not be good for us I don't guess. Drinking in the afternoon can be a problem."

When they arrived at the saloon they found there was hardly anyone in there, just a couple of men at a table and three girls who worked there. They stepped up to the bar.

"We'll each have a whiskey, but only one each," said Crawford.

Instead of drinking them down, they took their drinks over to a table and took a seat.

"Well Toombs, it didn't work out too well, did it?"

"Nope, I guess not. She just could not get back into the white world."

"I have known of white women who were brought back, and many of them, most of them I guess that I know about made the switch just fine. They was glad to get back to civilization and all."

"Maybe she was gone too long, and raising a son, and having him become who is now was just asking too much."

Crawford turned up his glass and drank it all down, and said, "She seemed to believe all this about her son being the mystery ghost. It's one thing to have yore followers saying such, but when a family member says it, well, I just don't know about that."

Sullivan drained his glass and answered, "I don't know. I'm not sure I want to know more than I already do. Know what I mean?"

"I think I do."

Twenty minutes later they walked back over to the hotel.

26

The Rangers sat around the tables in the hotel's dining room. They were always glad to be back in civilization, sitting at those tables, using nice forks and plates, drinking good coffee, and eating decent food.

After they finished eating some of them wandered off outside. Some went over to the saloon, others sat out front or stood around talking. A few turned in for the night early.

Captain Oliver Springtown was among the first to go upstairs. But before he left, he said to no one in particular and to all of them in general, "You boys enjoy a few days of rest. But remember the Major will send us back again, I am quite certain. This thing never ends, and won't never, I am sure, until the last Comanche is dead and gone to be with his fathers."

"Good night, Captain," several of the men said.

After a while Captain Springtown was followed by Ned Crawford.

"I'm goin' up," he said to Sullivan, as he stood.

"Think I'll stay down here a while. I'll be up later on."

"Fine, but don't wake me up with yore stomping around and dropping yore boots on the floor and all that."

"I will be as quiet as a church mouse."

"When I was a kid, I used to shoot mice and rats. I hated them being in the barn and leaving sign everwhere."

"I won't be leavin' no sign."

"Thank God for that."

Sullivan sat at the table listening to the stories the other Rangers told about fighting the Indians and chasing down bank robbers and killers. He knew these were brave men who would face anything to carry out their mission. They had been up against wild Indians, flooded rivers, burning heat, high winds, freezing northers, deep snow, drought, snakes, and then all of them had been in the war. They had managed to survive that and come back to Texas to jump right back into danger and death. He had to admit he admired them. And he was one of them now. Though he had mixed feelings at times, still he was glad he had joined up with them and that they had accepted him. Having listened to them for over an hour after the meal was finished, he decided to go up to bed.

"See ya in the morning, Georgia Boy," one of them said.

"Yeah, I'll be here. Good night."

Sullivan slowly walked up the stairs and turned left to go to the room he shared with Crawford. When he got to the door, he found something unusual.

There was a raw-hide rope tied to the door handle and reaching up to the top of the door and over it, the other end being inside the room. What the hell is this, he thought. He tried to open the door, but it was jammed by the rope. He pushed several times, and then put his shoulder into it and managed to open the door. But there was some heavy weight on the door as he opened it up further.

He stepped into a pool of blood running all over the floor. He pulled the door back some and saw Ned Crawford hanging on the back of the door. His clothes were all off. He had long and deep cuts on his arms and legs and all over his body. His throat was cut and his scalp had been taken. Blood was all over his face and had run out of every cut.

Sullivan was in shock as he stood there looking at what was left of his friend. The mystery ghost was all he could think of – Nacona Pledger. If you see him it is too late.

Now Sullivan was growing weak in his knees. He felt sick, and did not know what to do. He had to sit down, sit down on the bed for a minute before he fainted and fell over in the running blood. He could not stand to look at Crawford, yet he could not take his eyes off him.

He had to tell someone, run get help, alert all the rest. But it was too late to get help, no help would help Ned at all. Yes, he thought, I'll get the Captain who is just a couple of doors down the hall. He went out of the room and down the hall to the Captain's room, and there he saw on the door handle a raw-hide rope that ran up to the top of the door and inside the room. He forced the door open and found Captain Springtown hanging on the other side. There was blood everywhere, and the Captain was cut up in the same way Ned was.

He ran back down the hall to the stairs and yelled downstairs, "Get up here!"

The Rangers came running up the stairs and found Sullivan leaning against the wall. He said to them, "Look in both rooms, Ned and the Captain."

"My God," was about all any of them could say.

In a few minutes Captains Long and Trumbull came upstairs. They looked in the rooms and at both bodies.

Finally, Captain Trumbull said, "Somebody cut'em down. Go get the undertaker, and somebody go get the Major."

The next afternoon a wagon carried both caskets out to the cemetery. Then some of the men took the caskets up to the two graves dug side by side, but before they got there one of the Rangers who had gone on ahead came back to Captain Trumbull, and said, "Captain that woman done been dug up. Her casket is sittin' over there on top of the ground and she ain't in it."

They knew instantly what had happened. But that would have to wait. They had to lay to rest their friend and one of their leaders.

Reverend Walcott Jenkins was there with them to conduct the double funerals. He was as shocked as the Rangers at what had happened, but tried to give them some peace of mind about the destination of their companions. Major Henderson Pendergrass spoke about the two Rangers they were laying to rest. Reverend Jenkins said a brief prayer. It was quickly over, and the Reverend Jenkins walked away.

As the Rangers stood around, Toombs Sullivan said loud enough for all of them to hear, "Vengeance is mine, thus saith the Lord."

Major Pendergrass said, "Get things ready tomorrow, and then go after him the next day."

"No!" Sullivan protested. "We have to go after him now! He'll be gone and we'll never find him. In two days his tracks will be old, dust blown over them."

"You can't go off half-cocked."

"I am going right now."

"You'll have no supplies with you."

"I'll grab something from the hotel."

"All right. But you leave sign enough for the men to follow you."

"I will," Sullivan said as he turned and walked way.

The other Rangers shook their heads. One of them said, "That Georgia Boy is a fool."

"I heard that!" Sullivan said, not looking back. Maybe he's right he thought. Yes, he was a fool, a crazy fool now who had just gotten a gut full of the ghost, the mystery, the mad killer. There was only one way to deal with him, and that was to track him down while he could, kill him, skin him either dead or alive, and put his skinless body where all his followers would find him. And there was no waiting until supplies could be gathered. The Texas Rangers wasted too much time getting ready. He was ready now.

27

Toombs Sullivan walked into the hotel kitchen and said to Dottie Whitehead, the cook, "I need food for a few days."

"I can put some ham between some biscuits. Got a half an apple pie, and corn fritters and some cheese. Nothing else is ready for supper."

"Good, I'll be back down in a minute."

He went up to his room, changed clothes, put some other clothing items, extra ammo, and soap and a razor in his saddle bags. He picked up two canteens. Then he buckled on his belt, stuck his pistol down under it, and picked up his rifle. He took one final look at the door where he had found his friend. Gone now where his mixed feelings and emotions about killing the Indians. Yes, he would do to this Indian what he had done to Crawford and Springtown. He once again felt a perfect hatred boiling deep down in his heart and soul. He walked back down to the kitchen and put water in both canteens. He thanked Dottie Whitehead for the food and put it in his saddle bag.

Sullivan left the hotel, walked down the street, around the corner, and entered the livery stable. He saddled his horse, rode south out of town, and cut over near the cemetery where he looked for unshod horse tracks. He saw there were two Indian ponies, one for Nacona Pledger and the other for Caroline Pledger. That would slow him down some, but still he had a good start ahead of him. He followed the tracks, and headed toward the brush country.

The trail headed south but west of San Antonio. This was Comanche country. Sullivan had been through there before, but never alone. Was he being foolish? He did not care. He was full of so much hatred that he felt he could live on it, thrive on it, and from it gain an advantage over this would-be mystery ghost Indian. He had finally decided that the man was a coward. He was never seen for a reason. He led raids surrounded by hundreds of Comanches, but when they were over, he simply disappeared. That must mean something, Sullivan thought. It must mean he would not approach anyone head-on, face to face. That was about to change. Only in the dark of the night did he surprise Crawford and Springtown, when they least expected anything unusual.

The pony tracks were easy to follow and that caused Sullivan to wonder why. Nacona Pledger was making no attempt to hide his trail. It was so obvious that he was wanting to be followed, knew someone would follow, and that he must be waiting out there somewhere for whoever the unlucky person was. That caused Sullivan to stop and get down off his horse.

He knelt down and looked closely at the tracks. Then he looked up straight ahead. What is he doing? Where is he headed?

Sullivan mounted his horse again, he gently touched his sides with his boots, and said softly, "C'mon, Boy."

He looked straight ahead and always at both sides as well, looking for any movement of any kind. He kept listening for the birds. As long as he heard them but never saw any flying suddenly, he felt he was safe. Any change, any unusual sound, any silence, any movement meant there was danger ahead. He looked for rising dust and no dust at all. He looked at the tracks and in places where there were no tracks.

The light was fading now, the sun sinking deeper and deeper in the west beyond the hills. Sullivan found a place to camp under a tree. He tied his horse, took the saddle off, and with his blankets made a place to sleep. He built a fire, ate one of the biscuits with the ham in it, and ate half of the apple pie half, saving the rest for the next day. He drank all of the water in one of the canteens.

It was dark now, and the fire was almost out. He picked up his rife, and then walked quietly about fifty feet into some brush where he would not be seen. He sat down and leaned against a small tree. He would wait for the ghost Indian to appear out of the shadows, and then he would kill him. He would skin him the next morning, and then scalp him. Maybe he would put his skin and scalp on one of the ponies and the skinless body on the other. Then he would send them away so the Comanches would find what was left of him.

He looked up at the sky and saw every star that was up there. The moon was high and the night was almost lit up by it. He could see his saddle and blankets clearly. He would have a good shot at the mystery ghost. It would be no mystery after that. No more talk about the ghost. All the stars were blinking, far away and far above in the black sky. What would he do with the bodies? He did not care about Nacona Pledger. Just leave him where he lay, or yes, put his body on a pong, skinless, but the woman was white. He couldn't do that to her, even if she did claim to be an Indian, an Indian who hated whites. How many stars are there anyway? There must be thousands at least. Just look at them . . . .

And he heard his name being called. At first the voice seemed to be far away, and yet it was clear and distinct. There was no doubt it was his name he heard. How could this be? Then he felt the cool and quiet breeze fall gently across his face. It seemed to stay there instead of going on further. The limbs moved only slightly, and the tall grass that was ready to be cut into hay moved slowly to one side and then back up. He saw her far away down by the river. She was waiting for him, waiting for him to come to her, but there was something that kept him from being able to get up and move. He felt tied down, yet there were no ropes on him, nothing to hold him back but his own inability to reach out to her and find her. And then she was fading away, moving further away, further down the river, and then she was gone, gone away forever . . . .

The noise jolted him, causing him to almost jump. It was an owl near by. It was a good thing he heard him. Going to sleep out here a man could wake up dead, he thought.

It must be very late. Why isn't he coming? He should be here by now.

Sullivan felt the warmth of it all over his body, more and more of it. He opened his eyes, raised up quickly and looked around. The sun was up now and the world was coming alive again. And he was still alive, even though he had fallen asleep, no mystery ghost had appeared. Maybe this would be the day.

28

It was almost noon when Sullivan saw the buzzards circling in the sky. He stopped, pulled his rifle out of the scabbard on his saddle, got off his horse and slowly walked forward. Soon he found a dead Indian pony. He wondered if it was one of Nacona Pledger's. He began looking around and saw a rock ledge on the side of a small hill. There was a place carved out or washed out from under that ledge. There were tracks around it in the dirt, fresh ones it appeared. They were obviously Indian moccasin tracks. Some Indian had been there and done all this, whatever it was. Several large flat rocks had been placed over something up under the overhanging rock ledge. He pulled one of them back, and saw there was a body wrapped in blankets. It had to be Caroline Pledger. He decided to look no further.

He walked over to the dead pony. It had been shot in the head just under its left ear. There did not seem to be anything else wrong with it. Apparently Nacona Pledger did not want the extra pony to slow him down, but if these Indians valued horses so much why would he kill this one? It made no sense. But then maybe it made sense to an Indian. Perhaps he wanted it to look like he intended to travel faster, but was really setting a trap out there waiting on him some place. He knew he would have to be extra cautious.

Sullivan got back on his horse and followed the tracks he saw, always looking ahead, always listening intently, always looking to see what he would not normally see.

Surely that Comanche knew he would be followed. By now he knew about the Ranger's sense of justice and yes, even revenge. Surely he understood he could not get away with what he had done.

The sun was burning hot now. Sullivan could see the heat rising in the distance as he kept riding south across this waterless almost barren land. He thought he would be at the Hondo River soon if he and his horse could just hold out. He lifted his second canteen to his mouth, turned it up, and drank down the last small bit of water that was left.

Late in the afternoon he knew he was getting close to the river. He began to see the small trees growing along its banks. Then he saw the smoke rising from a small fire.

Someone was camped along the river. He got off his horse and slowly walked toward whoever it was, his rifle in his right hand, his horse's reins in his left. He stopped and tied the reins to a small tree. He slowly crept along, hoping to see who it was. He had to be Nacona Pledger. But why was he camping there? Had he completely forgotten that he was going to be followed? It must be a trap, the trap he was already expecting. Stop, slow down everything, do not even breathe, and try to relax, if that was even possible. Perhaps he should go around to one side or the other. If he did that, he would walk right into him, but which was worse, doing that or moving straight ahead, slowly, slowly? So, he crept along, and then he saw him.

It was the face of a white man, a face he knew from before. It was William Peele.

Sullivan called out to him, "Hello the camp! I'm walkin' in!"

Peele stood up and said, "You're one of the Rangers."

"I am. Name's Toombs Sullivan. What you doin' out here?"

"Just lookin' for more of my cows. They wander off or the Indians get them. Ain't sure this time what it is. So how ya been doin'?"

"Fine. How's the boy and the wife?"

"They're doin' well. I ain't sending that boy out after no more cows. Learned a lesson the hard way. How's yore friend that was with you that day ya'll brought Tommy home?"

"He's dead. That Indian called the mystery ghost came into Austin and killed him and our Captain right there in their hotel rooms. Then he stole away the body of his mama who had killed herself. We rescued her, but she didn't want to live in the white world. We buried her, and he came and got her. I found her back up the ways where he buried her. She was under some blankets in a crevice under a rock ledge. He killed the pony he carried her on. I found it all to be strange."

"That's the Comanche way of burying their dead. When one of them dies another takes him out on a pony. They find a place to bury him, maybe in a cave, or a deep place in a gorge. They wrap the person in blankets, and then they cover him with stones. They shoot the horse. All a part of the ceremony. I don't know if the horse is no longer worthy after carrying the dead or what. Maybe the dead needs the horse for a ride on the other side. These Comanches value their horses, so they take one with them so as not to have to walk no place. It might be a long journey, and ya don't know until you go. Know what I mean? But don't try to understand savage ways."

"Speaking of savage, what are you doin' out here, especially alone?"

"I can't hold up in my house. We got to keep on living. I got to get my cattle back. I can't just give in and give up, savage or no savage."

"I understand, I guess."

"About them two Rangers that got kilt, what was it like?"

"You know by now what the Comanche does to a white person. It was the bloodiest thing I ever saw. He tied them up on the doors of the rooms, and then he proceeded to cut them all to pieces, scalps gone, all that."

"Yep, it figures. So, what you doin' out here alone?"

"It was gonna take two days for the other Rangers in Austin to get ready and get goin' down this way. I came alone against good advice to see if I could catch up with that red devil. And I hope they catch up with me. I been tracking him since Austin when he left there in the night. Don't guess you seen nothin' of him and no other Indian?"

"No. I ain't seen nothin', and I ain't seen no sign either. Course I ain't been looking for nothin' but cow sign, so I wouldn't have noticed no pony sign I don't reckon. So, you got an axe to grind, so to speak?"

"So to speak," Sullivan replied.

"I got an axe to grind."

"I know."

"Spose we grind them together, and I go along with you? Two axes are always better than one."

"Are you sure?"

"Yep. We'll swing by the place and I'll tell the wife. We'll need to take some food with us. She'll gather up somethin' to see us through. I'll load up some extra ammo and all. You can't have enough or be too prepared when yore out in this country. Ya don't never know what to expect or what might happen. I have learned that since we been down here. This is a hard country to survive in."

"I've learned that much already, Mister Peele. I don't see how you can get on out there by yoreself. It takes a mighty brave man to do it."

"And a mighty brave woman too. I got one. I do."

"What about yore cattle?"

"They ain't goin' nowhere. They'll be here when I get back."

29

It was past dark later that day when the two men arrived at the Peele ranch. Mrs. Peele heard the horses and came out the door with a double-barrel shotgun.

"Ma, you remember this Ranger. Sullivan is his name. He's after the leader of them Indians who killed our boys. I'm goin' with him. We need some food to take with us."

"Sounds mighty dangerous, but I know ya'll know best. I'll get some stuff ready for ya."

"He did to that other Ranger that was here and a Captain what they did to our'n. We got to put a stop to that."

"Well, ya'll can kill him, but there'll just be another, more and more. They ain't no stoppin' them people."

William Peele went inside as Sullivan stretched his legs outside, and then led both horses over to a trough where they could drink. He knew the woman was right. There would always be more, but this one they could stop. Maybe.

Peele and Sullivan put up the horses in the barn. Then they went back inside to eat supper. After the meal they sat in front of the fire for a long time as the Peeles talked about their boys who had been killed. Tommy went to his room early. He did not need to listen to his folks talk about it the way they did every night. It was more than he could stand, and more than they could stand, but somehow the rehearsing of it all may have helped them cope with it. At least they hoped so. Sullivan did not want to hear it, but he would not dare tell them that. He had already seen enough and heard enough and experienced enough. He turned in, knowing that night in a soft bed would be his last for a while. He wondered if it would be forever.

He woke up in the middle of the night, and then fell back asleep slowly . . . .

He walked along the river and looked for her by the trees, but she was not there. He listened for her to call his name, but he heard nothing but the faint sound of the birds far away. The water flowed slowly down the bed of the stream as he watched it go away to some unknown place. The breeze blew the dead leaves from the trees and they gathered on the ground, then rolled toward the water's edge . . . .

Peele and Sullivan were up at dawn. They drank coffee and ate quickly the hearty breakfast Mrs. Peele had prepared for them. In twenty minutes, they were on their way riding hard after Nacona Pledger. They cut back over to the Hondo River and Sullivan picked up his trail again.

Early in the afternoon they pulled up their horses when they heard dogs barking, several of them. Then they heard shots. They looked at each other, and rode toward the sound of the gun-fire.

They came to a man who was yelling, "Genesis! Exodus! Sinner! Come heah! Heah! Heah!"

The three large hounds came running toward the man. He saw Sullivan and Peele and said to the dogs, "Down. Down." The dogs knelt obediently at his feet.

Sullivan spoke first, saying, "What is it, Mister?"

"Darn Indians stole two of my steers. They's a camp of'em on down I ran up against yesterday. Those two followed me back here, I guess. They must be hungry. If they'da axed I might have give one. I missed both of'em."

"A camp? How many?"

"Oh, I don't know. A bunch of'em, I know that."

"We're following one who killed two Rangers in Austin. He thinks he's a mystery ghost."

"Oh, him. Ain't no mystery at all. He's just a big medicine chief with the Comanch. They like him for some reason. Funny thing is, he's half white. The Mex know him, deal with him all the time. They tell me about him. No, there ain't no mystery. He's just slick and all. He might be standing right over there looking at us right now. But we don't see him because we ain't as in tune with the land and nature and the moon and the stars as he is. He goes where he wills. He's like the wind that blows wherever it wants to blow and all you ever see is the movement of the leaves and the limbs, and you feel it on yore face. Next thing you know you are dead."

"Yeah, that's the one we're after?"

"You know this land down here?"

"I been here before. Can't say I know it, not like somebody who lives here."

"I live here. I know it. You want me to go with ya? If we can kill him it would greatly help me with my cattle."

"Sure. We'd appreciate the help. I'm a Texas Ranger, Toombs Sullivan. This is William Peele. He lost two boys to these red killers."

"Nice to meet ya both. I'm Joshua Overstreet, lately of the Army of the Confederate States of America, but I been here for going on twenty year, so yeah, I know this land."

"I'm curious about the names of your dogs."

"Oh, that. Well, Genesis and Exodus are very religious dogs. They are obedient all the time. Fine trackers, excellent hunters, and good with the cattle. They mind every word I say. They look to please me all the time. Great dogs. Sinner is their brother, but ya know they's always one in a family of boys. He is a sinner, so I call him Sinner. He reg'ly breaks most of the Ten Commandments. He is specially bad on breaking number seven. Look at him. Ain't his fault he's hung like that. He's just a dog, that's all. Now tell me about the boys and the Rangers."

"We'll tell ya tonight. That is, if we camp and if we are still alive. If we ain't it don't matter. But we better get goin'."

"My horse is right over here. Genesis, Exodus, and Sinner! Heah! My horse is named Stephen Austin. Everything and everybody has got a name. And a name ought to mean something, not just a tag that was put on ya or yore dog or horse for no good reason. They ought to be a reason for a name."

Peele and Sullivan looked at each other and smiled. Then Sullivan said, "So why did ya name yore horse Stephen Austin?"

Joshua Overstreet looked puzzled, and then answered, "I'll be dog-gone if I know."

Overstreet was a big burley man. He wore a red checkered shirt, brown baggy pants held up by suspenders and stuffed in his floopy looking boots, and a black floppy hat that sat back on his head. That being the case, his face was exposed to the sun always and was a dark tan. He had several day's growth of dark beard. He was loud and boisterous, but was also a friendly sort. He had a Navy pistol in a holster at his right side and another stuffed in his belt on his left side. He had two large knives, probably Bowie knives, but only the handles could be seen, and one was in each boot on the outside of his legs. He was well prepared for anything that came his way.

His horse was loaded down with two full saddle-bags, one tied on top of the other, and also a couple of blankets tied in front of them just behind his saddle. He had four canteens of water. In his scabbard on the right side of the horse was a Sharps rifle, and a shot-gun in a scabbard on the left side.

He climbed up on his horse and said, "Let's get goin', Boys."

30

The three men rode hard after the Indians who had taken the two steers. Their trail was easy to follow, and they were not far behind them. Soon they saw them ahead of them about three hundred yards.

Sullivan stopped his horse, pulled out his rifle and fired two shots, missing the Indians both times, but they abandoned the steers and fled on south. When they reached the steers, they stopped for a moment.

"What ya want to do with them?" Sullivan asked.

"Leave'em here," Overstreet replied. "Let's get after them savages. I'll pick these boys up later. They won't go far."

They followed the Indians further on, but were not able to gain ground on them. Sullivan's fear was they would soon meet up with that larger group and their camp Overstreet had spoken of. Soon they reached where they had been camping for a few days it appeared. They stopped, dismounted, and gave the horses and themselves a rest.

The three dogs began running around the camp-site. They were nervous, darting in and out from one side to the next. They sniffed the ground and pawed, digging here and there.

"How many ya think were here?" Sullivan asked both men.

Overstreet walked around looking at the still smoldering fires, the pony tracks, the Indian's footprints, and places where there had obviously been tents. He looked down toward where the Comanches had gone.

"Oh, I'd say twenty-five or thirty. They got some women and children with them. If ya look at these tracks all over you can clearly see that. So, they ain't a large number of warriors, I don't think, maybe twelve or so. They left out from here this morning sometime."

"Ya think Nacona Pledger is with them?"

"Hard to say. I did see some footprints that are larger than all the others. His daddy was a chief called Big Man, sometimes called Big Medicine. He was known for his size. They say the mystery ghost is even larger than his daddy was. So that could be his tracks I seen."

The words caused Sullivan to grit his teeth and strengthen his resolve to give Nacona Pledger the justice he had coming to him. He was not far away. They would catch them soon, if not that day, then surely the next.

They mounted up and rode on, knowing the main band was at least a half a day ahead of them.

Soon the dogs began barking and ran away from the men. They looked like they were hot on the trail of game, but it was the Comanche scent they had picked up.

"Genesis! Exodus! Sinner!" Overstreet called out, but it did no good. The dogs were gone. "We better hurry," he said.

Two minutes later they heard shots. Overstreet tore out ahead of Sullivan and Peele, obviously concerned about his dogs. Then two of the dogs came back to them.

"Genesis, Exodus, where is Sinner? Where's he at, Boys? Go find him."

They rode further as the two dogs ran ahead, and Overstreet began calling out, "Sinner, come forth from thy hiding place! Sinner! Where art Thou!"

The whining of the dogs told them where Sinner was. They found him dead from a gun-shot. Overstreet quickly jumped down off his horse. He held the dog like a mother holds a child. He cried and buried his face in the dog's neck.

When Sullivan and Peele dismounted and walked over to Overstreet, he said, "It done got personal now. It's one thing to steal a man's cows. I can understand a hungry man, but to kill a man's dog just ain't right."

Sullivan replied, "I'm sorry about this. I guess I got ya into this and cost you your dog."

"Nope. I come of my own accord. It was Sinner's fault. He was headstrong always. Couldn't hardly never do nothin' with him. But he loved me, would even die for me and he did. It would have happened somewhere some time along the way. It was just the nature of sin. It catches up with ya. A sinner takes his chances, and Sinner took his, that's all. I'm gonna bury him. You two go on, and I'll be along right soon. Me and Sinner just need a little time together, if ya don't mind."

"I understand. We'll be after them, but we won't be hard to find."

"I'll find ya. Won't take me long. He just deserves that I treat him right now and not leave him out here for the varmints to get at him."

"All right," Sullivan said.

Then Peele said, "I understand very well what ya say. Ya got to take care of yore own, even yore dog. Well, Mister Ranger, let's go on after them."

"Right. Right."

Sullivan and Peele mounted up and rode off, not wanting to leave their new friend, but also not wanting the Indians to keep gaining more ground on them.

They had not gone far when an arrow flew between them. Sullivan pulled out his rifle and charged off after a Comanche who had jumped on his horse and darted off to the right of them. He fired twice at him, then stopped his horse, jumped off, knelt down, and fired a shot at the Indian's horse. The horse tumbled forward, throwing off the rider. Sullivan got back on his horse, charging after the Indian who was now running without his bow and arrows, but he turned around, pulled out a pistol and fired at Sullivan. Sullivan pulled up his horse, and shot the Indian in the chest. He fell backward, dead immediately.

When the two men walked over to the Indian, they looked closely at him. He had another pistol in his belt, along with a knife. He wore a bullet belt over his right shoulder down across his body.

Then Sullivan knelt down, pointed to the man's chest, and said, "Look at that."

He also wore a Texas Ranger badge.

Sullivan took it off and put it in his left shirt pocket.

"Next to my heart," he said, as he looked up at Peele.

31

Sullivan and Peele followed the Indian trail another ten miles when suddenly it turned to the west. They got off their horses and looked at the ground and the tracks.

"What are they doin'?" Sullivan asked.

"They're goin' into Mexico. They think we won't go on after them."

"They're right. At least I won't. I got no authority to go into another country, don't matter who it is or what they done."

"Well, this is the end of it then, but we ain't to the Rio Grande yet. Let's go after them. Maybe we can catch'em."

Sullivan and Peele rode on and reached the river as the sun was setting beyond it. They got down off their horses and began making camp for the night. An hour later Overstreet joined them.

"What ya'll doin' just settin' here?" he asked.

"I can't go any further. That's another country over there," Sullivan replied.

"Put yore badge in yore saddlebag and let's go."

"I like my job and the pay. If I put my foot over the line, wherever it is, middle of the river or wherever, then I get fired."

"Who's gonna know?"

"My Company will be here along with two others probably tomorrow. I'm gonna just sit right here and wait on them."

"I'm goin' on after them."

"It's suicide, one man after all them."

"One man and two hellacious dogs."

"Don't do it."

"It's been nice, Gentlemen. Genesis, Exodus, ho the river!"

Sullivan and Peele watched Overstreet as he went across the river and disappeared into the lengthening shadows of the trees on the other side. His dogs were right behind him.

"He's in Mexico now," Peele said.

"I hope we see him again."

"And his dogs."

"Yeah, the dogs."

"I'll see if I can get some wood for a fire," Peele said.

"Good idea."

When the fire was burning, they made some coffee and heated some beans. They ate biscuits and dried beef. After they were finished Sullivan took the pans and tin plates to the edge of the river and washed them. He took off his boots, sat down, and soaked his feet in the water. Then suddenly from behind him came Peele without a stitch of clothing on and waded out into the river.

"I think you'd be legal right here!" Peele called out.

"Sounds like a good idea."

Sullivan undressed and went in the water, and suddenly felt clean all over, but not on the inside.

Later that night both men lay on their blankets looking up at the stars. Neither said anything.

Sullivan did what he did every night. He thought of Constance and their son, and his thoughts drifted away to a place back home and now gone. Even though life had been hard, it was all they knew. They knew they were happy at the time, and he valued that beyond all other things . . . .

The thunder woke him up and the lightning flashed across the sky as the rain poured down on them. It was a blinding rain that came down in torrents. He looked out at the river, but could not see it at all. He tried to cover himself as best he could with his blanket, but it was no use. It was too late and he was soaked already. The night was black except for the flashes that lit up the sky and everything around them. In those moments he could see a little. He thought he heard the splashing of a horse, and then hoof beats on the bank of the river. The lightning flashed and he saw something briefly, but he could not tell what it was. Then suddenly it was on him almost. It was an Indian on a horse. He jumped off the horse and came running toward him, and it was the biggest Indian he had ever seen. He could tell that much each time the sky lit up. But he seemed to be running in slow motion, running hard, yet moving slowly. He knew who it was instinctively. It was Nacona Pledger. He had a spear in one hand and a tomahawk in the other. He was going to kill him before he could get awake and reach for his pistol. Where was it? He couldn't find it. He saw the lance coming right at him and tried to jump . . . .

He looked at the river when he sat up with a jolt. The bright moon was reflected on the water. He looked around. Peele was sound asleep. He had been thinking about Constance and the boy, all he had, and all he lost when he drifted off to sleep. And now life was what it is today, just today is all he had, and with the darkness now surrounding them, there was the hope of tomorrow. And the little fire finally went out.

32

"I'm headin' on back," Sullivan said as he and Peele saddled their horses. "I'll meet the other Rangers and save them some miles and some time. No use just sittin' here and wonderin'."

"Guess you're right. What about Overstreet?"

"I hope he never found them. He wouldn't stand a chance."

"Ya tried to warn'im. All's a person can do."

They rode together for a long time. Then Peele cut off headed for his place. Sullivan continued back-tracking hoping he would run into the Ranger companies. At mid-afternoon he found them.

"The prodigal son has returned," Captain Pete Blankenship said when Sullivan rode up to him and the two other Captains. "I was given Springtown's job. Jack McAllister is now the Sergeant. What'd ya find?"

"I found a few who had stolen some cows. That Mister Peele went with me, and we came upon a man named Joshua Overstreet. They was his cows that was stole. We got the cows back, but they killed one of his dogs. He and the other two dogs gone into Mexico off to the west across the river. We spent the night by it, and then come on this morning."

"He went after them into Mexico?"

"Yes, Sir."

"How many is he chasing?"

"We'd found their camp. We figger about twenty-five, but maybe only a dozen warriors."

"Oh, well. He should do fine. If they don't skin him that is. What about Pledger?"

"We think he's in that bunch. There was a lot of sign around where they camped. Overstreet said he is a big man with big feet that make big tracks. He declares he's along with them others."

"Gone to Mexico, eh? Well, that does it if that is the situation. We'll have to wait for him to come back into this country. And he will. Sooner or later, he will. There's too much temptation here for him to stay away. Besides he thinks all this land is his and we stole it from him."

The three Ranger companies turned around and headed back north-east toward Austin. They made it to San Antonio for the night, and stayed in the same hotel. They ate the same food and drank the same whiskey. Then they went on toward Austin the next day.

When they arrived at Ranger headquarters the three Captains went into see Major Pendergrass. They took Sullivan with them so he could report on what had happened.

After Sullivan finished giving his account of what he had seen, Pendergrass thought a minute, and said, "We'll have to just wait it out then. But we can't sit around waitin' for the Comanche to decide to do some more meanness. There's too much other stuff goin' on. I'll have orders for each company in the morning. Get some rest, but be ready to go tomorrow."

The four men acknowledged what Pendergrass said, got up, and left the room.

When they stepped out on the sidewalk Captain Blankenship said to Sullivan, "Want to go get a drink before we eat supper?"

"Thanks, but I'll pass this time. I need to do a couple of things."

"All right. See ya later."

Sullivan went into the hotel, stepped over to the desk, and said to the clerk, "I need a different room."

"We cleaned that room up real well, Mister Sullivan. You cannot even tell there was ever anything that took place in there."

"You can't clean me up. What happened in there is in me, and always will be. And I need to get all my stuff out of there, so I need two keys."

"All right, Sir, sure, sure. Here's your key to another room and here's your old key. This new one is fine, fine indeed."

Sullivan took the keys to both rooms, and decided to go first to the one across the hall. He walked up the stairs, turned left, put his saddlebags on the floor, and opened his old room. He went inside and looked around. He gathered up all his clothes and other personal items, taking them to his new room. He looked around in that room, and thought this room is not fine, fine indeed as that man said. It's just a room, that's all. But for Sullivan it was a room with no memories. He had too many of those and was tired of them already.

33

Each Captain was to meet separately with Major Pendergrass to receive his orders. The next morning Pete Blankenship sat nervously across from the major's desk. He was a big man, tall, filled out, muscular, which is one reason he had become a sergeant. Besides the men liked him, though they had no idea he would ever be their Captain. His imposing size and presence made him a natural leader.

"Pete, I'm giving you and your men a dream assignment.

There's a bunch of wild men made up of Comancheros, white crooks, thieves, and killers, some Mexicans I think, and some Indians that's been raiding down around Victoria. They robbed the bank there in town, and have been stealing horses and cattle. They killed a few ranchers. The law enforcement people there can't do nothing with them, and have asked for our help."

"I thought you said a dream assignment?"

"I did. It's a bad dream assignment. Nobody knows where they are. They're just ravaging that whole area. Go down there and put a stop to it any way you have to."

"All right, Sir, we'll do our best."

"That's why I picked you and your men."

That night Captain Blankenship had his company come into his hotel room where he told them about their new assignment. A couple of men sat in the only chairs. Others stood around the walls of the room. Two sat on the edge of the bed. Toombs Sullivan sat on the window sill. Several of the men smoked cigars or cigarettes they had rolled.

"Well, Boys, he gave us a tough one this time."

"They're all tough," said Bill Blount.

"Yeah, I know. But that's what we signed up for and get paid all this money for. We're goin' to Victoria. Ought to take us about three days or so to get there. There's a wild gang of marauders down there – Indians, Mexicans, whites, Comancheros. They robbed the bank, killed some people, stole cattle and horses. We're goin' to find them and put a stop to all this. Our horses need a day of rest and feedin' and we do too. So, take it easy tomorrow. Rest up. Clean yore weapons, re-stock what ya need. We got four new men comin' to join us as replacements. Any questions? I need a drink. I'm buyin'"

The men followed Blankenship out of the hotel and across the street to a saloon, The Western Star. When they went inside, they lined up along the bar. Glasses were placed in front of them and each glass was half filled with whiskey. Blankenship stood in the middle of the line. He lifted up his glass.

"Here's to Victoria," he said as he drank its contents down, as did the other men.

Sally Hamilton walked up behind him, tapped him on the shoulder, and said as he turned around, "So who's this Victoria?"

"She's a queen, Sally."

"Oh, really?"

"Yeah, the queen of the low-lands down near the coast."

"That Victoria? You had me worried there for a moment."

"Oh, Sally, you know you're the only one."

"If only that was true."

Sullivan and the other men then went to sit down at tables, leaving Captain Blankenship talking with his admirer.

"How about a friendly card game?" Willard Boyd said.

"There ain't no friendly card game," replied Bill Blount.

"We'll play just for fun."

"It won't be no fun when I shoot ya."

The other men at the table laughed.

Boyd looked at Sullivan and said, "How about you, Georgia?"

"Not me," Sullivan answered. "I don't want to shoot you either."

As the men laughed again, Sullivan stood up and said, "I'm turnin' in."

When he approached the door, a young woman named Lydia Langley stopped him and said, "What's your hurry?"

"Who said I was in a hurry?"

"Well, you're leaving it looks like to me."

"That I am."

"Why don't you stay around?"

"Why should I?"

Lydia Langley was an attractive woman. She seemed taller than most females, had a nice figure, distinct facial features, a small dimple on her chin. Her red hair, curled up on top of her head, called attention to her.

"You could stay around and buy me a drink."

"Oh."

"I could buy you a drink."

"I had a drink."

"Have another. Two whiskies," she said over her left shoulder.

"All right, since you put it like that."

They set down at a table near the door.

"I've been seeing you around, Mister Ranger."

"I've not noticed you."

"I know, but you should have. You're not married, I gather. Have you ever been or do you have a woman somewhere?"

"No and no, and I don't want one."

"My name is Lydia Langley."

"I'm Toombs Sullivan."

"I know it. I know who you are. I know you are from Georgia, and came here sometime after the war was over. Right?"

"That's right."

"I came here from Mississippi during the war. I was raised up in Vicksburg. I had a cousin who lived here, but when I got here, I could never find her. I don't know what happened to her."

Toombs Sullivan turned up his glass, drank down the whiskey, and said, "I can't help ya with that."

Then he stood up and walked out of the saloon.

Lydia Langley said, "You are one strange man, Toombs Sullivan."

34

The new men were Clyde Benning, Tom Hall, Johnny Adams, and Calvin Ricketts. Both Benning and Hall had been Rangers before. They had gone off to the war and survived it, then came home to Texas and declared they were through with all that. They wanted to make a lot of money. They went in together and bought some land where they tried ranching, but had little success. So, they came back to the Rangers and asked for their old jobs back. They were given them without hesitation. Johnny Adams and Calvin Ricketts had come to Texas after the war was over. They were both from Alabama, but when they returned home after the war, they found there was little to come home to, so they left. Like Sullivan, they had no idea what they would do in Texas, but going there seemed like a good idea. They would figure it out when they got there. But nothing had developed for them. Being used to regular meals they began looking around, deciding a regular job was better than no income at all. Out of desperation they joined the Rangers. They were all introduced to the others first thing on the morning the Company was heading out to Victoria.

When Company D arrived in Victoria, Captain Pete Blankenship went into the office of the town marshal. The other

Rangers stood around outside sizing up the town. A few of them sat on wooden benches along the front of various stores, while others stood against the walls or walked around trying to regain some feeling in their lower portions. Toombs Sullivan spied a general store across the street, and said to Willard Boyd, "Come with me."

When they entered the store, Sullivan walked over to a glass covered display of various kinds of hard candy. The man who ran the store saw him and approached him.

"What can I do ya for?"

"I want some of this candy, a bag full."

"Which ones?"

"That one. That one. That . . . . Oh, just mix it up."

The man picked up several of each kind, and said, "Will there be anything else?"

"That'll do it."

"You gents Texas Rangers?"

"Yes. How did ya know?"

"You got that look. All of you do, ya know. Plus, I saw you ride up while ago. You couldn't be nobody else."

"That obvious, eh?"

"Yeah. We've been needing you folk here. These raiders are looting, stealing, killing. They have to be stopped."

"That's why we're here. What can ya tell us about them?"

"They're the worst kind of killers there is. That's all I know."

"We'll do what we can. How much I owe you?"

"Twenty-five cents ought to cover it."

Sullivan paid the money, and he and Boyd walked out on the sidewalk. Sullivan put two pieces of candy in his mouth, one on each side, and handed the bag to Boyd. When they reached the other side of the street, he took the bag back, and then handed it C. W. Pickles and said, "Pass it around, Boys."

The Rangers took the bag of candy and stuffed their mouths and pockets. When they handed it back to Sullivan it was empty.

Soon Captain Blankenship walked out of the Marshall's office, and said, "Gather round."

When they had all come together Blankenship said, "All right, here is what I found out. This band of killers hit a ranch south of here yesterday and killed the owner, a man named J. K. Longbaugh. They took his wife and his daughter who is about fifteen. We need to go see if we can pick up their trail and go after them. Maybe we can save the women."

"What are the odds of that, Captain?" asked Boyd.

"What is wrong with you? What you got in yore mouth?"

"Candy."

"Oh, I was afraid you had two bad teeth. I was gonna pull them for ya. I'd say the odds are not great based on what we have seen and what we know. We'll go out to that ranch and see from there what we do. Let's mount up."

Almost an hour later they came to the Longbaugh ranch. They found the house and the barn had been burned down, and there was still a little bit of smoke rising from both.

They dismounted and began walking among the ruins, looking for anything that might be of help.

"Don't see nothing, Captain," called out Sergeant Jack McAllister.

"I was afraid of that. Which way do the tracks go?"

"Straight south. Maybe five or six unshod Indian ponies and lots shod horses, Longbaugh's amongst'em I assume."

"Let's go after them. Mount up, Boys?"

The Rangers rode off in pursuit, and soon came to what was left of the Longbaugh herd, at least part of them. They found about thirty-two of the cattle had been killed and skinned. It also appeared a good many others had been driven on south.

"Drivin' cattle will slow them down. Let's get after them. Pickles to the point! Go find them!"

C. W. Pickles spurred his horse, and rode off leaving a small cloud of dust.

The Company then followed the tracks of the raiders, each man growing more and more concerned about the fate of the two women. It was unlikely they would be able to find them in time to save them, even if they caught up with that band at all. They knew too well what those kinds of people did to women. But still they rode on.

On and on they rode, mile after mile, dust upon dust, thirst and sweat and heat and a scorching sun. Buzzards were in the sky and wild burrows ran away. Lizards and snakes crawled under rocks. And the taste of the dust was in their mouths, and dust was in their ears and noses, dust was in their eyes.

How in God's name do people live out here, Toombs Sullivan thought. What a God-awful place this is.

35

C. W. Pickles came back to the company a couple of hours later and made his report.

"I found where they camped last night . . . . and I found the women, Captain. It ain't even human what they did to them. They was raped, split open, skinned, and scalped."

Captain Blankenship looked distressed by what he heard. He thought a moment, and said, "That's what they usually do. So, it ain't no surprise. Well, Boys, it'll be dark soon. Let's make camp here, and in the morning, we'll go hard after them. They still following cows, Pickles?"

"Yep. They don't look to be in no hurry. They're camping too by now, so we can get on them pretty quick I would think."

They made their camp, tied off their horses, set their saddles down where they would sleep, and started fires. They made coffee and ate what food they had with them. They had cut some beef off one of the cows and hoped it was all right to eat. But when they looked closer at it, they knew it was a silly idea.

Sullivan lay awake a long time that night. He did not want to go to sleep. He did not want to dream about Constance any longer. It made him feel too bad when he woke up. He would rather not see her at all, and besides in his dreams she had finally left him. He knew she would not come back. He did not want to dream about the flowing river, which he could not identify, and willow trees and hay fields blown by the winds. He did not want to dream about going there to meet her, and then have her not show up. She was not showing up any more. It was over and done, so let it rest, and sleep no more. But what about Little Toombs? He never saw him in his dreams either, and he wondered why.

But there was always the war. There had been times when he had dreamed about the war. He had seen all of its horrors many times over. It was not enough to live through that. Any man who was there had to take it with him the rest of his life, and he could never get away from it. It was always there with him. Why couldn't the war be like Constance and just go away?

Just before the sun came slipping up over the eastern horizon, the Rangers were up gulping coffee, eating a little dried beef, and saddling their horses almost all at the same time.

They mounted up and Blankenship said, "Awright, Pickles will lead us to where the women are. Boyd and Blount, you stop off and give the women a decent burial and say some good words over them. The rest of us will pursue the savages, and you two catch up to us when you can. Let's go!"

The Company rode hard toward the south. When they came to where the women were now baking in the morning sun, they stopped for a moment. The Rangers could hardly stand to look at them, but they did. They did not want to smell them, but they did. They did not want to think about what had been done to them, but they did. Blankenship pointed toward them, and then led the Company off further as Boyd and Blount dismounted. Pickles rode on ahead to find the gang of killers.

By early afternoon the Company spotted Pickles waving them on forward. When they reached where he was, he pointed to a cloud of dust and said, "Just ahead!"

In a few brief frightening moments, they came up behind the raiders and began firing their pistols at them. Those in the rear turned around very much surprised, and began drawing their pistols and their rifles. A few fell off their horses to the ground. Others returned fire, hitting no one.

Suddenly there was a stampede as the cattle and horses all began charging forward together. The dust rose up in the air, making it difficult to see who was who. Cows and horses and Indians and Comancheros and Mexicans and white Texans and Texas Rangers were all together racing all out. The Rangers fired at them and they fired back at the Rangers as they could.

Toombs Sullivan was in the middle of it all, surrounded by Rangers, cows, horses, Comancheros, Mexicans, Indians, and the whites. He quickly emptied his pistol and jammed it back under his belt. He pulled out his rifle and began firing it. He knew he killed four or five at least, but in all the confusion it was hard to tell.

Then the killers began to pull away, leaving the cattle and their dead and some of the horses. The Rangers were clogged up, unable to move fast enough because of the cattle that now surrounded them.

When they finally became untangled, they chased the killers for several hours, but were never able to get close to them again.

After many miles the trail they left suddenly turned west, and they knew they were headed for Mexico.

With the sinking sun the Rangers made it to the Nueces River, where they camped for the night. They built a couple of fires, made coffee, heated their meals, and sat around the fires eating. Boyd and Blount soon joined them.

"What now, Cap'n?" asked Roscoe Pride.

"We keep after them, but we prob'ly won't catch'em, unless one or two of them have a horse that goes lame. We'll see how it goes. We'll go all the way to Mexico I guess."

"Why don't we just go on over after them?" Tom Hall asked.

"Because we got no authority to do that. Agin the law."

"Who's gonna know it?"

"I will, and I report to the Major. I can't look him in the eye and tell him a lie. Sergeant, post a guard. Better get some sleep, Boys. We'll go hard in the morning."

36

With the morning sun the Rangers were after the killers again. Toombs Sullivan was given the point for the second time. He was not sure he knew the land well enough to do it, but at the same time it was a sign that he had been accepted and trusted. The lives of all in the Company were in his hands in a way. He thought he could do the job, but also made sure he was both fast and careful, a combination not easily accomplished.

He rode off on his own, wondering if one or more of the killers might be out there waiting for him. It was just a chance he had to take. But still there could be one waiting on him, or maybe more than one. What if he actually caught up with them, all of them, caught up with them before he even realized he was on them? Oh, that would be fine, a fine howdy-do. What would he do then? He had to be careful, very careful, but he had to move on out. He had to get out ahead of the Company in order to protect them. That was the only way to warm them, be far enough out front to find that band before they all got up to them without warning.

Sullivan was all eyes and ears, looking at the ground in front of him and then out beyond him. He listened intently, often stopping for a moment to see if he could hear anything. He was nervous, tense, afraid, unsure of himself, but at the same time it made him completely alert. He was prepared for whatever happened. He held his Henry rifle in his right hand. Now and then he checked to see if he still had his pistol stuffed down under his belt.

Sullivan kept thinking, don't they know we're back here? Do they really think we would give up or just go away? They have enough contact with us to know we are still coming. They must know that. Maybe they think they can get to Mexico before we catch up. They know we will not go over there after them. So that's their plan, ride hard and straight west, cross the river, and they'll be home free.

In spite of his fear Sullivan kept after them. He was determined to find out where they went. Following the trail of the killers was not all that difficult. The tracks of the twenty to thirty in that band were easily seen, still a mixture of shod and un-shod horses. But after almost three hours he began to notice something he had not expected. He saw it nine or ten times. He decided he needed to get back to the company and report what he had seen.

He turned around and rode hard back over the trail he had been following. This could be very important. It was totally unexpected, and made absolutely no sense at all. But nothing out here made any sense. Nothing in Texas made any sense.

When he approached the Company, Captain Blankenship held up his hand and stopped the column.

"What'd ya find, Sullivan?"

"A strange thing, Cap'n. I began seeing where a horse or two would turn off to the right by itself. After maybe ten of those I realized they were all headed north. I didn't know if maybe they would double back around and come up behind me or the entire Company later on. Thought I better let you know about it."

"I don't know what they might be up to. But I guess we'll find out soon enough. Since you been on their trail, you go on now and see if you can find'em. We'll be right along, not far behind ya."

"Awright, Cap'n."

Sullivan turned around and headed back where he had just come from. As he followed the same tracks he had followed earlier, he kept trying to understand what was happening, and what these people must be up to.

He passed the place where he had stopped and turned around. Still he saw the same pattern, a horse or two every few miles turned north, while the others continued west. After a while it looked like he was following only five or six horses. Then he came to a place where they seemed to stop, for how long he did not know, but then all the remaining horses in the group turned north.

So, it wasn't Mexico after all. They were stringing the Rangers along, and all the while they were all headed to the same place with some of them getting there sooner rather than later. What were they planning now?

Sullivan got off his horse and began looking around at the tracks. They were now all unshod horses, Indian ponies, and no shod horses. So, the Mexicans, whites, and the Comancheros had all gone north earlier, and maybe all these now going north were Comanches.

Five minutes later the Company arrived where he was standing.

"This is where the rest of'em turned and went off up that way, as you can see."

"What in the devil are they doing?" Blankenship asked.

"They're not just running from us. That's pretty obvious. Fact is, they don't seem to be too concerned about us being after them. Maybe they think we ain't no more. There's a number of ranches and home places up that way, we know that. Since they lost the cattle and horses they had when we was chasing them, maybe they're wantin' to replenish what they lost."

"God, I hope not. But you might be right, Sullivan."

"I'm afraid I am."

"Me too. Ransom Pride, take the point!"

"Sure, Captain," Pride said as he rode off headed north now.

"Captain," Sullivan said, "you ever seen anything like this before?"

"No, never. Everything I see most ever time we come out is somethin' I ain't never seen before. This is a land of surprise. Everything is the same and everything is a big surprise. It's what I love about Texas. I ain't never been bored since I became a man. There' always something new."

"I'm not easily bored. I don't need a lot of surprise to make me happy."

"Anybody make you come to Texas?"

"No, Sir, can't say they did."

"Anybody making you stay?"

"No, no, I am on my own in that."

"Get used to it then. Let's go, Men!"

37

As the Rangers began trailing the killers again, now it looked like those who had left the group were coming back to it. One by one horses from the east were joining them as they moved to the north. Maybe the ones that had come from the east had just been sitting there waiting on the others to come by. It was difficult to tell. But in these wide open spaces they could easily find each other from some distance. This also meant that Ransom Pride would be able to see them far away which was helpful. They could also see him however.

He followed their now widening trail, easily seen in the dirt. He could see their dust in the distance, which made him think they did not know he was behind them. They really must have concluded the Rangers had given up trying to catch them.

He rode over a little rise and saw an Indian pony standing by itself. That was odd and unexpected. He did not know what to make of it. He slowly approached the pony, looking around to see if its rider had perhaps been wounded earlier and finally died and fell off, but he saw nothing. When he reached the pony, he got off his horse, walked up to it, and then saw footprints around it. They were made by moccasins and not boots, just what he expected. He walked thirty feet following them, and suddenly out from under the sand an Indian jumped up in a cloud of dust and shot an arrow through his chest. Ransom Pride fell backward and hit the ground.

He looked up at the sun. The sky was clear and the sun was bright. It was such a hot day and the sand was hot. He could feel it burning through his shirt. A man could die of thirst and from the heat if he stayed out in this too long without his hat on. Where was his hat he wondered? What just happened? The pain was burning in his chest. What was that?

Suddenly there was shade over his face, a welcomed sight. Any relief from the sun was good. But who is this? It's an Indian like the ones he had been chasing. He looks like a Comanche, and he smells like one. They have that wild odor about them. What is he doing grabbing my hair?

The knife was plunged into Pride's stomach, his chest, his throat was cut. Then he was scalped. There was no time for all the other things Indians normally did to people.

The Indian lifted Pride's hair into the air and let out a yelp. Then he looked around for Pride's horse, but it had already gone back the other way. The other Rangers would find it soon. The Indian jumped on his pony and rode off.

It was not long until the Rangers saw the horse coming toward them.

"Grab him, McAllister!" Captain Blankenship shouted.

The horse was captured and the Rangers gathered around it.

"What the heck?" Blankenship said. "Any blood on it?"

"No, not a bit," McAllister replied.

"This don't look good. I got a man killed."

"Weren't yore fault, Captain."

"Let's go find him – and them."

"I'll go out ahead!"

"No!" Blankenship said. "That got one man killed already. We'll all go face it together this time. Somebody bring along Pride's horse!"

They proceeded north and soon came to the place where they found Ransom Pride. They dismounted and stood around him. He was covered in blood, the top of his head being a bloody mess. His throat was nearly severed into. His stomach had been sliced open from his naval up to his sternum.

No one said anything until Blankenship spoke somberly, "Somebody get a couple of shovels. Let's give him a good burial, but make it quick. We got to catch'em. Somebody get that arrow out of him and clean him up a little."

Toombs Sullivan did not move. He did not help dig a grave, nor did he help get Ransom Pride ready for it. It was not that he was shocked or surprised by what had happened and what he was seeing. He was beyond all that. It was just the savagery of the land, not just these killers and the others. There was just something about the country that screamed out terror and horror and naked aggression. It was not safe anywhere, not down here in this brush country, not in a hotel room in Austin, not over near the coast, not even in the first place you come to in Texas, the town of Marshall. And no kind of person here was ever safe, not a rancher and his family or a woman in her house or boys chasing cattle or a Texas Ranger out in the country or in his hotel room. The whole state of Texas seemed to breed violence and killing and stealing. There was not a man or woman or child or horse or cow or dog that could find any sense of security in this place. Is this what he wanted to find in Texas? Surely not.

Soon the grave was deep enough to put Ransom Pride in it and get enough dirt over him to keep the varmints from digging him up.

Sullivan watched as some of the men wrapped him in his blanket, lifted him up, and carried him over to the hole in the ground. They gently placed him on the ground, and then looked up at the Captain.

The Captain read from his Bible the Twenty-third Psalm.

Then he said, "We lost a good man today. He did his duty and did it well, as always. It was just his bad luck that I sent him out ahead. It could have been any one of us that went like that. Maybe he could have prevented it. Maybe he never had the chance. Maybe he wasn't careful enough. We don't know and never will know. It don't matter now. What matters is for the livin' to take a lesson here. Whatever he didn't do, the rest of us have to do it, whether it's being more careful or more alert or more dangerous to the enemy. Let's all learn a lesson here, like I just said, but I don't know what the lesson is really. Maybe it will be revealed to us as time goes on. Anyway, that's it. Pray. Oh God, take our brother to you and yore kingdom. Amen. Cover him up, and let's get goin'."

38

The Rangers followed the Indians' pony tracks the rest of that afternoon. They could get no closer to them, especially since they had paused to bury Ransom Pride, but what else could they have done? They could not have just left him lying there in the dirt.

Finally, not long before dark they could see the smoke from a fire in the distance and how it lit up the sky. They stopped to look for a moment.

"Whose place is that up ahead?" Blankenship called out.

Toombs Sullivan moved up closer to him, and said, "That would be the Boutwell place."

"Com'on!"

The Rangers rode faster now, and in a few moments could see the flames still burning the house and barn. They rode right up to the house, but it was too late to do anything. The damage from the fires had been done.

They dismounted, tied their horses back away from the fires, and began looking around. Their guns were at the ready, not knowing if there might not be a Comanche still there, or more than one. Some of them had their Sharps rifles, while others had one or more Colt pistols in their hands.

"Spread out, Men," Blankenship said, "and be careful."

Then they saw Jim Boutwell with his arms tied to a limb of a tree on the other side of the house. He was totally naked, his stomach sliced open, part or his skin had been removed, probably before they killed him. He had also been scalped and his genitals were hanging from his bloody mouth.

Jesse Boutwell was lying nearby. She was also naked, and it appeared she had been raped several times, probably in front of her husband. She had then been sliced open and scalped.

"Find the Claxton girl", Blankenship said somberly.

The men spread out and began looking for her, but could never find her. After several minutes they all came back together.

"Captain, it looks like they took her captive for the second time," Sergeant McAllister said.

"I think you're right. We should have figured that. They probably came here just to get her, just to show us they can do what they want and get away with it. And the Comanches must have broken off away from the rest of them. This is what they do, but not those others that were with them. How did we miss that along the way? Awright .... let's get these people in the ground. Then we'll make camp here for the night."

Several men took shovels from the pack mules and began digging two graves. When the Boutwells had been placed in them and covered over with dirt Captain Blankenship read from the Bible, said a prayer, and then they all walked away without saying anything.

The men were quiet for a while. They seemed stunned, though they had seen this many times. It was something they could never get used to no matter how many times they witnessed such savagery. They watered their horses, and set up camp away from the house. By then the flames had died down at the house and the barn. Smoke still rose from both and would most of the night. They gathered what wood they could use and started a couple of fires.

As they ate their supper they began to engage in conversations, but it was all small talk. No one mentioned anything they had seen or heard that day. After they ate, they began smoking cigars and making cigarettes. A few of the men had brought along small bottles of whiskey. They passed those around, sharing what they had.

"Sullivan," said Andy Wilford, "You plan to be a Texas Ranger all yore life?"

"I didn't plan on being one at all to begin with."

"You just happen into it?"

"You might say that."

"I did say that. It was Springtown that got ya into it, right?"

"Yeah, he did. What about you?"

"I been wantin' to be one since I was about twelve year old. So, I got started, but then the war and all. You know how that was, and what it did to a man's plans for hisself. Did you have a life back in Georgia?"

"Yeah, I had a life, but not much of one. Got tired of workin' for other people. When the war came along, I just jumped right in. I didn't care if I lived through it or not. I had nothin' to go back home to. That's why I was so careless in the war. But I could never get myself shot. I lived through it, and as soon as it ended, I lit for out some new place. I wandered around Alabama and Mississippi for about a year, then came to Texas as an afterthought, so to speak. It was an accident that I wound up here."

"So, my first question. You gonna always be a Ranger?"

"I am tonight and I will be tomorrow, but beyond that I got no idea. You?"

"I will always be one. Here, have a swig of this."

A wide black blue purple sky covered over them. It seemed like in all directions it never ended. A million stars winked down at them. Now and then one would race across the sky, beginning some place no one could even imagine and falling out of sight some place where no one had ever been or would ever go. The vast spectacle of the night sky made the earth seem so small and insignificant, and each man seemed to be of no consequence. They all felt it in one way or another, and no man dared to speak of it. The stars and the moon, now rising, had always been there and always would be, and they were only passing through for just a brief time.

Toombs Sullivan thought about all he had seen, the friends he had made, and how they had been killed in such a god-awful land. Measured against the sky above and all the stars in the universe, what were any of them? How important were any of them, and were they important at all? It was all temporary, nothing lasted, nothing counted, nothing was important . . . .

And the breeze played on the leaves of the trees by the river. The water in the river moved so slowly that it seemed like it did not move at all, this river that began nowhere and ended in the same place. The tall grass slowly leaned back and forth like waves on the ocean. The scents of honeysuckle and gardenia drifted by and enticed his nose, each one seeking dominance over the other. The songs of the birds signaled that all was well. He had met her there, and he expected to find her again, to smell her flowing hair, to see deep in her eyes, to touch her lips.

But there was no one there now. He stood there alone. She was gone, gone forever, and only the memory of her remained, a faint memory of a face he was beginning to lose, a face he could hardly recall. Where had she gone, and what would happen to the life they had shared . . . .

"Get up, Men! We got to go get with them killers as soon as we can. Coffee is made, grab some quick, eat up quick. Let's go!"

39

"Today, like we ended yesterday, nobody rides point. We are all point together. They know we are after them, I think. Well, at least they must know we're coming along. So, we stick close. Keep yore eyes open at all times and yore ears. Keep yore guns at the ready. All right then, let's head out."

The Rangers continued traveling north, following pony tracks which were easy to see. There was one shod horse also. That must mean the Claxton girl was on it. But where were the others that had been with the Comanches? They just slipped away somehow.

Toombs Sullivan thought about how the pony tracks were together that day. There was no attempt to hide them or spread them out. That must mean the Comanches were being deliberate in the trail they left, and maybe that meant they were wanting a fight. He pulled up ahead near Captain Blankenship.

"Captain, these tracks all together like this must mean they want us to see where they're going. So, you think maybe they are waiting on us out there to catch up?"

"You're thinking like a Ranger now, Son, and a Texican. Of course they are. Trouble is we know that and nothing else. We don't know where they'll be and won't until it is too late.

By the time we find out their bullets and arrows will already be whizzing by us."

"I sure hope they are by us and not in us."

"Me too. Keep steady."

Near noon they paused to rest their horses. Just as they dismounted, suddenly from in front of them and from both sides there came a hail of both bullets and arrows. Ten or twelve Comanches, no one could tell how many for sure, charged up near them, shot at them again and quickly rode away.

Several Rangers fired back at them, but did not hit any of them.

"Everbody all right?" Blankenship asked. He looked around quickly. They were standing again, for some of them had dropped to the ground.

"Nobody hit, Captain," McAllister replied.

Sullivan stuffed his pistol back under his belt, took a deep breath, and looked at his horse to be sure he was all right.

"How many ya think?" Blankenship asked.

"Must have been about ten, at least, I'd say, but it happened so fast I couldn't really tell," McAllister said.

"There must be forty of fifty or more in that band. We don't really know, but they sent back or dropped back these ten or so to hit us. That means they will be up there and try it again."

Sullivan then asked what he had been wondering about, but had not wanted to mention yet, "Captain, what about Nacona Pledger? Ya think he's leading that group?"

"The mystery ghost could very well be with them. Being always a mystery, we won't know until we see him. But no one has ever seen him, no white man, except those that were about to die. So even if we see him, we won't know it's him, I guess. I don't think he was with that band at Victoria. He and some others must have joined them later, if at all.

"Now this time we ride differently. Instead of two columns I want us to be in a knot with three rows of four across. I'll be out in front. Immediately drop down, turn and fire if they attack when we are mounted. If we are dismounted, stay in yore group and look around carefully, always at the ready. Let us proceed, Men."

Now the Rangers moved out in their new formation. They were slower and even more cautious. They were constantly looking ahead, to the left and the right, and also behind them, expecting anything anywhere anytime.

They scanned the horizon in four directions. There was no dust anywhere, no sign of any group up ahead. This was both good and bad. It could mean they were not close to them now. It could also mean they were already lying in wait out there.

With the sleeve of his left arm Sullivan wiped his face as best he could. He could feel the sweat running down his back, his shirt already wet. He licked his lips and tasted the dust. He tried to spit, but there was not much that would come out of his mouth. He took off his hat and gently knocked it against his right leg. A little dust flew up and was carried away by the light wind that blew from the east.

The Rangers were still moving slowly as they advanced. They were in no hurry to get where they were going or to engage the enemy no sooner than they just had to. That would come soon enough. There was no need to rush into something when they had no idea where it would be.

Like Sullivan, all of them had a thousand thoughts rushing through their minds. What was it really like to die? Would it hurt very much? Would they be dead before some Comanche started removing their hair? How painful would that be? Maybe these questions would be answered soon, too soon.

"What are ya thinking, Sullivan?" asked Andy Wilford, over his shoulder and to his right.

"I'm thinking this might be that day I mentioned to you last night."

"You mean about leavin'?"

"Right, or maybe leave by getting' myself dead out here with the help of some Indian."

"Would that be so bad? You sounded like you was wanting to die last night, die in the war."

"The war is over now. I wanted a Yankee to kill me the decent way. No Yankee ever took any scalps that I know of. That would not be decent to have my hair lifted either after I was dead or before I was dead. It don't seem fittin' to me. It is a savage thing to do to a body."

"These people are savages. What ya expect?"

"We better shut up and watch out."

40

Fifteen minutes later an arrow came from the right and went through the neck of Tom Hall, one of the new Rangers. He had been on the outside of the last row, with Sullivan next to him. Sullivan had been riding with his rifle sitting across his saddle and his right hand on it with his finger on the trigger, holding his reins in his left hand. He turned quickly and fired into the back of the Indian who had turned to ride away, and was fifty yards from them at least by the time Sullivan fired. The rest of the men dismounted quickly. Sullivan remained on his horse and rode out a ways to make sure the Comanche was dead, and also to be sure there were no others.

When he came back, he found the men gathered around Tom Hall. It was a terrible sight. Hall lay on his back on the ground with the arrow in his neck, a foot of it all the way through. Blood had run out of his mouth and down the right side of his face. His eyes were still open revealing the shock of what had happened.

"Break it off and pull it out of him," Blankenship said. "Tie him to his horse. We'll bury him later. We can't keep taking time for this."

Three of the men hoisted Tom Hall up and laid him over his saddle. They tied a rope to his feet, threw it under the horse, and then secured him on the other side. The Rangers then mounted up and rode on further.

Soon Toombs Sullivan pulled up alongside Blankenship, leaving his spot in the formation.

"Captain, they're gonna pick us off one at a time like this. How about me and one other go out along to the right of us a hundred yards or so and two others out on the left? We hit them before they hit us."

Blankenship held up his hand and said, "Hold up! Sullivan has a better idea. He and Boyd are going out to the right a hundred yards, and Wilford and Blount, you go out to the left. You'll get behind them maybe and hit them first. All right, go at it."

The four men rode out to their positions, and they and all the others proceeded to move forward.

As Sullivan and Boyd took their places, they turned their attention to the horizon while also carefully looking at every yard of ground in front of them, looking for tracks to see if a pony had cut in toward the others. Sullivan was nervous, trying hard not to miss anything. Boyd kept looking off to the right to be sure there was no Indian out beyond them. Twenty minutes later Sullivan spotted a Comanche hiding behind a large clump of brush. They had come around behind him. Sullivan held up his hand and pointed at him. He put his rifle to his right shoulder, aimed carefully, took a breath, breathed it out slowly, and gently squeezed the trigger. The Indian flipped forward off of his pony.

Sullivan and Boyd rode up to him. Sullivan got down and rolled the Indian over on his back. He had a knife and a Colt pistol under his belt, a string of beads around his neck. He wore a blue shirt and leather pants. He had a leather band tied around his head. There was a scalp tied to his belt. His Sharps rifle lay on the ground beside him. His bow and a sheath of arrows were around his neck across his back. Boyd rode up closer to him and spit on him. Sullivan got back on his horse and on they rode.

Sullivan killed one more this way a while later, and Wilford did as well on their side. By then the Indians had figured out what the Rangers were doing and attempted their tactic no more that afternoon.

With the lengthening shadows of the evening The Rangers stopped to make camp, and also to bury Tom Hall. They gave him the usual brief service.

"Anybody know much about Tom Hall?" Captain Blankenship asked at the beginning of the service.

Johnny Adams spoke up, and said, "Yes, Sir, I know a little. He come here from Mississippi. He was chasing a dream, Captain. He wanted to get rich in Texas, like so many others who come here. But the war called him away, and he was glad to go fight. He was quite a soldier. He started out as a private, but became an officer by the time the war was over. He was a good man who loved his mama. That's, that's about all I know, I guess."

"No finer words can be said of a man than that he loved his mama. A man that loves his mama makes a good husband and father, and has respect for all women and children. Too bad he never had the chance to show it."

With that Blankenship read the twenty-third Psalm and said a prayer. Then he said, "Okay, cover him up. Then get with the camp."

They set up their camp, built a couple of fires, and prepared their meal. Blankenship posted a guard as the men settled down to try to get some sleep. But sleep was far from the minds of all of them, even though they were tired from their journey. They wondered if the Comanches would come in the night, if the mystery ghost would appear, if some wayward arrow might strike them while they slept, and they thought about revenge. They thought a lot about revenge.

The Rangers had lost too many friends now, to say nothing of what they had seen done to the families they found butchered. They did not talk openly about that very much, mainly because it was not a very enjoyable thing to do. But deep down inside of each of them the fires of revenge were smoldering.

They would find a way to ignite those coals into raging flames, and let those fires run free across the land. It was their job to keep people safe, but at that point they felt like they were not doing a very good job of that. They were not even keeping their own men safe. But each one of them knew they were reaching the breaking point. How much longer it would take they did not know. They just knew their time would come someday. Someday they would put a stop to this current madness.

41

The Rangers rose with the rising sun, rekindled their fires, drank coffee, and ate quickly. Sullivan walked over to Captain Blankenship.

"Captain, I got a theory about why we are now just following Comanches, if that is indeed what we're doing."

"Spit it out."

"Well, Sir, just maybe those that were splitting off and going north were Comancheros and Mexicans. Maybe they then circled around to the east and then went south. Maybe more Comanches came from the east and joined the band as they went straight on north where we saw tracks coming back in from the east, ya know. And we ain't seeing nothin' now but unshod Indian pony tracks. That would explain a lot about their killing of that family. It had to have been just them alone when that was done. The Comancheros and Mexicans would not do that to nobody it seems to me."

"I think you just may be right. I'm afeared you are right. That means the Comancheros and the Mexicans were then free of us and could go on raidin' out to the east and south while the Comanches are taking us on a wild goose chase, a wild Indian chase."

"Yes, Sir, that's the way I see it."

"We'll worry about them later. First thing we got to do is catch these Comanch."

"You mean kill'em don't ya?"

"That's exactly what I mean."

"Well, guess what, Captain. They will lead us on a while and then they'll cut west to Mexico, and there ain't a thing we can do about it. Just another dead-end chase."

"I know it. You got any better suggestion?"

"I didn't until you asked me. But it just came into my head. What if we stop chasing them north and instead go north-west trying to beat them to the border?"

"That ain't a bad idea at all. But what's the chance of us gettin' to the place where they'll cross? It's a long shot at best."

"That's true. What if we put riders out maybe a mile apart? They can spot'em maybe, and then come signal us all to come together. If they go in about, oh I don't know, a few miles from the river, then they'd have time to get back to the main body of us."

"All right, we'll try that, and you'll be one of the spotters, since it's yore idea. Let's get goin' men! We got a new plan of attack. Gather around and we'll tell ya about it."

The men came together and Captain Blankenship pointed to Sullivan and said, "Lay it out."

Toombs Sullivan explained his idea to the Rangers. Then he asked, "Who has any idea about where they might cross the river?"

No one said anything for a moment. Then Bill Blount spoke up.

"They'll cross at Eagle Pass."

"Why ya think that? And where is it?"

"The Frio River flows into the Rio Grande right there. They can have water all the way to the border that way. And there's a tradin' post there where they can replenish their supplies. You can bet they buy stuff there a lot. That's why they've never burned it down or killed any people around there. There's about five hundred people in that settlement. That's the best place for them, if ya ask me."

"I did. And that makes sense to me. What about it, Captain?"

"I think Bill has a good idea. Sullivan will be in charge of the out-riders. He'll pick 'em. This may not work, but there's not much else we can try. All right, let's get goin'."

The Rangers loaded up, broke camp, mounted up, and rode hard toward the north-west and the river crossing at Eagle Pass.

Toombs Sullivan kept hoping his idea was not some hair-brained fantasy. He did not want to lead the Rangers astray. It was a gamble, but, yes, that was their only chance. They would never catch them if they kept following their tracks north. Is Eagle Pass really the place? Maybe so. They could just as easily choose some other place to cross the river. But the idea made sense, especially the part about the trading post and their need to re-supply themselves. How could any white people trade with these savages? Don't they know what they do, how vicious they are?

All of these thoughts kept going around and around in Sullivan's mind. It would not be long until they would find out if he was right.

Bill Blount, since he knows the area, Billy McCary, Andy Wilford, and Willard Boyd, these are the ones he would choose. Counting himself that would be five, and should be enough.

42

Toombs Sullivan figured he and the other four must be about two miles from the river. He could look to his left and see Blount, and then look to the right and see Boyd. It was difficult in the now bright sun of late morning, but he could tell where they were. Hopefully they would see the Indian band before they were seen by them. If not, then that would defeat the purpose of what they were trying to do. Then when they saw them, they would dash back to the company as quickly as they could.

Sullivan got down off his horse to stretch his legs for a few moments. It had been a hard ride to get to the river and then get in place. They had paused at the river just long enough to let the horses drink water and eat a little of the grass that grew at the edge, but that was it.

Now it was back up on his horse. He had pulled his binoculars out of his saddlebags. With them he began scanning the horizon. It was barren looking. He could see the waves of heat rising, and imagined he saw large bodies of water in the distance. This only made his thirst even worse. He put the strap of his binoculars around his neck, and pulled his canteen off his saddle horn. He turned it up and took a long drink, knowing he need not be careful to conserve his water. In a little while he would be back at the river for more or he would be dead and not need any at all.

The late morning turned into the afternoon and that wore on with no Comanches in sight. Hours passed as the sun began easing low in the western sky.

Then Sullivan saw two horsemen coming toward him at a fast pace. He waited and looked as they drew closer. It was Bill Blount and Willard Boyd. When they pulled up it was Boyd who spoke.

"Sullivan, I decided to go on further north a ways. I went about two mile and found their tracks out there. They beat us here and done gone towards the river."

"We better get to the Company!"

Sullivan fired a shot in the air, knowing the other two men would come and join them at Eagle Pass. Then he, Blount, and Boyd headed out for the river.

In a few minutes they had crossed the two miles and found Captain Blankenship and the Company sitting by the river near Eagle Pass. Without dismounting Sullivan spoke to the Captain.

"Boyd found where they came by further up than we were ahead of us! They headed toward the river! They may be camped up there along the banks!"

"Mount up, Men! Let's go after them!"

The Rangers followed the river for several miles, finally coming to a place where there were a lot of pony tracks. They could tell that is where they crossed the river.

"Look, Captain," Sergeant McAllister said as he pointed across the river.

Then they all heard the Comanches yelling and laughing at them. They danced around, bent over pointing their rear ends at them, jumped up and down, shook their rifles and spears at them. Then several of them began firing their rifles in the air.

As Blankenship got down off his horse he called out, "Dismount and fire your weapons! Give it to them, Boys!"

The Rangers dismounted, pulled out their rifles, some knelt down, some stood erect, and they shot at the Indians.

They were well within range, but a little far to be very accurate. They dropped a couple of them, but most of the Indians drew back further away and took cover. But one of the Rangers did not shoot at them. That was Sullivan. He knew it was futile to even try to hit them. So, he just stood there watching.

"All right, Boys, forget it!" Blankenship said. "They're just too smart for us. They know we can't go over there after them. Did any of you see that young white girl or a big one that could be Nacona Pledger?"

The men shook their heads as a couple of them said no.

"I guess we failed this time. We'll get'em someday. Let's camp here tonight and we'll go to Austin in the morning. Sergeant, you and Sullivan go back into Eagle Pass and get us some supplies. Blount, take somebody with you and see if you can go get us some fresh meat. Maybe there'll be a deer coming to the river or somebody's stray cow."

When McAllister and Sullivan arrived at Eagle Pass, they went in the trading post.

"Howdy, Gents. What can I do for ya?" said a short middle-aged man with a white beard and hair that was about half white, more so around his temples and ears, and thinning out on top. He was standing behind the counter, and had a white apron on covering most of his faded red shirt.

"We need a few items," McAllister said. "I'll look around and then we'll need the usual, flower, salt, coffee, and we'll see what else."

Sullivan, as he and McAllister had agreed, walked over to the counter and leaned against it.

"You Boys be Texas Rangers I would assume."

"You would be right. Say, you ever see any Comanches come around here?"

"I hear they come near here, but I don't never see'em."

"Do they pay cash or trade things with ya?"

"Wh . . . . I said I don't see no Indians here."

"I been told they trade here with you, which is why you still have what hair you do have and why this place ain't been burned down. What you say to that?"

"I say I don't know what you getting' at."

"I am getting' at you not only see them but do business with them. We're trying to catch them, especially the one named Nacona Pledger. Now since we are after them, failing to give us information or telling us a flat out lie could lead to being arrested by us and taken to Austin. You can't lie to an officer of the law in the middle of a case or a pursuit like this. They crossed the river back up yonder a ways and are camped on the other side. We can't go get them since they're in Mexico, but we will get them one of these days. We will kill every one of them. I want to know if they come in here and if Nacona Pledger comes in here. Now I'll give you another chance to talk to me, yore last chance."

"Uh, yeah . . . . they come in here. I've known Nacona a long time. He comes in here. He's the big one, ya know. He's about as tall as the door there, huge. Lots of times he comes here by himself. Some of the time he comes with others or maybe he sends them in here. Their money is as good as anybody else's money. I'm here to run a business. I ain't no court of law. Besides I like my hair where it is."

"I think you're a lily-livered, yellow spined, money-grubbing, too bit coward, and no real Texan consortin' with the enemy. I think my friend needs yore help over there. I'm goin' outside before I shoot you between the eyes."

Ten minutes later, having gotten all they needed, they put the supplies on their horses, and started to mount up.

Sullivan said, "Just as we suspected."

43

At the river Sergeant McAllister reported back to Captain Blankenship, saying, "Nacona Pledger goes in that trading post a lot I would say. That owner calls him by his first name, and seems to know him well. Sullivan had to threaten to arrest him to get him to talk, but he finally did."

"But we still don't know if he's over there or not. If so, this is the closest we have ever come to him."

"Close don't count."

"No, but maybe next time. One thing we know for certain is that he'll be back. He can't stay out of Texas. He's like Grant in Virginia. He just couldn't stay away. He just had to keep on. That's Nacona Pledger."

"That ain't a comfortable way of talking, Captain. We know what Grant did in Virginia."

"The boys shot a deer. We got fresh meat. It's cooking, and will be ready afore long."

"Good."

The men ate their meal, then sat around the fire smoking and engaging in one of their favorite things, talking about the war, what happened, what they did, what they saw, but never how it affected them. By now, a year after the war was over, they had rehearsed their stories well, and each man already knew what the others would be saying. But that did not matter to them. It seemed to do them good to talk about it. Always it was on an impersonal level, just the facts, the action, the battles won and lost, and what they did in them. They never said anything about the suffering they saw, how men died, the friends they lost, and not much about what they did to Yankee soldiers.

The conversations died down, some rolled over and went to sleep, others looked up at the night sky, the blinking stars and the crescent moon. Others now and then looked across the river at the Comanche fires and wondered what they talked about at night.

Clyde Benning took the first watch. He was new to the company, but was well liked and seemed suited to the work.

He was in his mid-twenties, tall and lean, sandy-haired, and had a light-colored mustache. He had always been quiet, only speaking when spoken to, which is one reason he was thought well of.

With first light the Rangers began to stir. Sergeant McAllister was always the first up. He put more wood on the still smoldering fire, and put on the coffee. He looked around and did not see Benning, and wondered if he had come and gotten anyone to take his place.

As the men rose, he asked, "Where's Benning? Did anyone else pull guard?"

The men looked at each other, shaking their heads with a few saying, "Not me."

"Spread out. Captain, we don't see Benning!"

"Let's find him."

The men walked out in all directions, up and down the edge of the river, back away from it, looking, and calling his name. Sullivan found him off to the right of where they were near the river's edge.

"Over here!" he called out.

The Rangers rushed to where Sullivan stood over the body of Clyde Benning. He had his throat cut, his shirt torn away, sliced from his pelvic area up to his sternum, his stomach and intestines spilled out on the ground, his scalp had been taken, his ears cut off, and his eyes cut out.

Sullivan said, "Look at these footprints. Ever seen a foot that big?"

"Nacona Pledger," said Blankenship. "Look, he came right across the river, and then went right back. Benning never saw him."

They all turned and looked across the river. The Comanches had already left.

Then Blankenship said, "Now this is the closet we have ever been to him."

"Too close," Sullivan replied.

After a moment with no one saying anything, McAllister said, "The mystery ghost ain't no mystery no more. He didn't stay away."

"Let's get him in the ground," Blankenship said as he looked back down at Benning. "Somebody get a couple of shovels. You know what to do."

They buried Clyde Benning by the river, held the funeral service for him, and then loaded up and headed out away from the river.

Except for what was said at the service no one spoke a word, not as they loaded up, not as they headed out, and not for a long time as they traveled back to Austin.

44

"We got close, real close to him. He was just across the river, but he came in the night and killed Benning. We never even knew anything was going on," Blankenship reported to Major Pendergrass.

"We have to keep after him, this mystery ghost. As we all know, he'll be back in Texas. It's just a matter of being at the right place at the right time, a time when ya run into him. I was afraid you would come back empty, so I have a plan now to get him."

Major Pendergrass laid out his ideas about trapping Nacona Pledger. Then he said, "I'll talk to the other Captains. We'll get him this time."

"Oh, we will, Major. We'll get him. This cannot go unanswered, all the things he has done. We'll get him."

"Well, go on and get some rest. We'll talk more tomorrow."

"Instead of resting, I think I'll go join the boys and get a drink."

"Sure."

As Blankenship walked across the street and approached the saloon, he could hear the piano playing, the loud talking, and the laughter. When he stepped inside, he could smell the smoke and the aroma of whiskey. Most of the Rangers were seated at tables. A few stood at the bar, among them Toombs Sullivan. Lydia Langley was talking with him, and standing very close to him. Sullivan did not seem to be very interested in what she was saying.

Blankenship stood in the middle of them, and said, "Boys, gather around here as you can. I talked with the Major. He wants us to keep at it until we catch up with Nacona Pledger. We know all the killin' and stealin' he's done, and we're gonna catch him if it takes near forever. If possible, I want us to take him alive. We won't bring him back here, but we are gonna hang him by the neck until he's dead. And I want to hear him crying out for that slut mama of his and call on his fathers who went before him and beg the great spirit to rescue his sorry ass. Then we will hang him by the neck until he is dead."

Some of the men laughed, others nodded their heads, and all were in agreement that they would do whatever it took as long as it took to get Nacona Pleddger.

"We're gonna string that half-breed up and stretch him out. When we get through with him, he'll be tall all right.

He'll be about twelve feet tall if we could stand him up."

The men laughed again, as Blankenship said "Let's drink to that. That is worth drinking to."

At a table next to the back wall, Joe Joe Buffalo sat with his head down. He was slumped over the table. A near empty whiskey bottle was in front of him. He picked up his glass and emptied it into his mouth without raising up. He had heard every word that was said.

No one seemed to notice him. It was a common site to find him there when he was in town. He came around some, but few paid him any attention. No one ever asked where he went in those times when he was gone for weeks or longer.

"Now, here's what we'll do. Our three companies are going out again, but we won't be seen together. We will be the lead company. The other two will trail behind us so they won't be seen. They'll be a couple of miles back. One rider will be between us so he can hear if there is any gunfire. Then he'll fetch the two behind and they'll come chargin' forward, but more slanted toward the river in case they run for it. We'll try to catch them in a cross-fire if we can."

"How we gonna know when they come back into Texas?" asked Sergeant McAllister.

"They don't stay in Mexico very long. They run in and back out to their home land which is Texas. Remember this is what all this killin' is about, tryin' to run out the whites. They'll be back soon. And we'll be there."

"Where will we be, Captain?" asked Willard Boyd.

"We'll be along the river. We know some of the places where they cross into Texas. It's like trying to stake out an animal, a deer maybe. We know they like that area around Eagle Pass. That is the most likely place."

Joe Joe Buffalo had listened intently. He slowly rose up half way and backed out of the rear door that was near him. No one noticed that he had left. They would not have cared one way or the other if they had. After all he was just another drunken Indian or Mexican or half white or a breed of some kind and that did not matter at all.

"Any questions, Men?"

No one said anything.

"Awright then, get yore rest. Clean yore guns. Be ready, and we'll be going soon. I don't know when yet, but soon. Drink up. Again."

45

Two days later the three Ranger companies mounted up and rode out of Austin, with Blankenship and D Company in the lead. Three miles out of town the other two stopped and let D Company move out beyond them.

After three days of hard riding Company D was near Eagle Pass where they camped by the river. So far there had been no contact with the Comanches, which was all right since their plan was to draw them out from across the river. They would simply wait on them now.

The men were glad there was nothing happening. They were hot, tired, and dirty. They needed to rest. They set about making fires, watering their horses, bathing in the river, and cleaning the dust out of their weapons. Then they ate their supper which consisted of Jack rabbits they had killed along the way that afternoon, beans, and fried potatoes. The rabbits were roasted over the fires filling the air with the scent of fresh cooking meat. There was no breeze, so the smoke hung low over the camp. After the meal McAllister posted guards and set up a rotation schedule.

Tombs Sullivan was on the first watch just up the river from the camp. He was where he could keep an eye on the horses. He did not like the feeling he had about that night. Something did not seem right to him. He could not make out what was bothering him. Had they been spotted that afternoon or followed? Were they now being watched? He felt that was probably the case without question. He kept looking across the river trying to see into the shadows, looking for any kind of movement.

The other men felt the same uneasiness. The tension below the surface in the camp could almost be seen. Every time an owl flew near or a bird called out or a small animal scurried along by the river they looked up, ready to grab their guns.

The coyotes screamed out in the night. One close to them called out to others who came running to him crying and whining. The Rangers were used to them, and would have no problem sleeping through it. It was just a part of the night in a place like that.

At midnight they began hearing bird calls from across the river, fake bird calls, Comanche calls. Every man heard them since no one was asleep or would be that night. The Indians must have known that for they seemed to keep this up just to annoy the Rangers. Whatever their motive was it was working.

The other two companies were camped about three miles away. They would be ready early the next morning if Company D was attacked. As soon as that attack began, they would come riding in to catch the Indians in a vice grip. If the attack did not come then all three companies would move further south along the river, still hoping to draw out Nacona Pledger and his band.

After a long sleepless night, the light of a new day began to slip in from the east. First there was just a change in the sky, and then slowly streaks of light broke through the few rainless clouds that flitted by. Then bright rays of the sun cut through the limbs and leaves on the trees by the river.

The men were up and stirring about, having slept none and closing their eyes seldom. It was not long until the fires were started up again and the coffee pots hung over them, low over them so the fires would boil the water. Some of the men stood around with cups in their hands waiting. Others peed in the river, while still others went off on their own to find private places.

"Don't get shot in the rear!" they were warned.

Once the meal was over and everyone was ready to go, Blankenship called them all together.

"Well, Men, nothing so far. So, we'll move on along the river for a ways and see what happens. From all the commotion during the night we know they know we're here. Uh, Sullivan, you be our middle man today. Just stay about halfway between us and the other two companies. When you hear shots fired, you'll know what to do. Questions anybody?"

Company D moved south-east along the river while Toombs Sullivan rode back to meet Companies B and C. Captains Long and Trumbull saw him coming and moved out ahead of their men to meet him.

"News, Sullivan?" asked Trumbull when they met.

"No contact during the night or this morning. We're going on down along the river. I'm your go-between man. Keep an eye out. If you see me approach waving my hat that means come on along quick."

"We'll do just that."

Sullivan turned and went back to station himself about halfway between the companies. He was close enough to Company D to hear gun-fire and close enough to the other two to let them know it in a few minutes. Now it was a matter of waiting for something to happen. He wondered if the waiting was the worst part, but then the contact could be hell on earth, so which was worse?

46

Toombs Sullivan walked his horse slowly along trying to keep up with D Company, but also wanting to stay close to the other two companies. He had to be alert with so much depending on him and his reactions. If he failed to hear the attack on his company, they could be wiped out without ever receiving any help from the other two.

The sun climbed and the heat rose. The dust filled the air and buzzards flew above. The light breeze blew from the east, but the air was hot. Sweat ran down his face and the dust stuck to him. He drank water from his canteen, but it was warm.

The minutes slipped slowly by and the hours were like the days. He began to think . . . .

Suddenly shots rang out from behind him! The Comanches were attacking Companies B and C! There were vollies of shots, like nothing he had heard since the war ended!

He turned his horse to go to them, thought better of it, and turned again. He raced toward his company and fired two shots in the air to alert them.

Soon he saw them coming, and he shouted out at them.

"Gun-fire back there!"

"Let's go, Men!" shouted Blankenship.

They raced past Sullivan as he turned his horse and joined them.

In a few minutes they saw the Comanches on both sides of the two companies firing at them. Several of their horses had been shot, Rangers were on the ground shooting back, some of them dead already.

Blankenship and his men spread out and fired at the Indians killing some of them. Suddenly they all rode hard to the river and began crossing it with Rangers from all the companies after them. Three Indians were shot off their horses and hit the water. The rest reached the other side where they hooped and yelled and waved their rifles.

Then the Rangers saw him on his white pony. He was a tall figure astride his mount, sitting high on it. His long hair was braided and down along both sides of his chest. He wore a blue shirt and had a feather and bone chest dressing hanging from around his neck. He held up his rifle in defiance.

As the Rangers sat on their horses on the bank of the river, they heard Blankenship say, "My God."

"What is it, Captain?" McAllister asked.

"That tall one there is Joe Joe Buffalo."

"Joe Joe Buffalo? You mean he is Nacona Pledger?"

"I mean he is Nacona Pledger."

Sullivan was sitting beside Blankenship. He looked over at him and spoke.

"Captain, he was in the saloon the other day when we talked about what we would do. In fact, he has been around a good bit."

"He has always known what we would do and where we would be. We have had a spy in our midst, and not just a spy, but the big Injun himself."

"That explains a lot."

"Now we know. Awright, Men, there's nothing we can do now. They won't come back very soon and we can't go after them. So, let's gather our dead and wounded, and take them back to Austin."

The three companies had lost five men in the surprise attack. They went back over to the site of the battle, a hundred yards from the river, and dismounted. They began looking after those who had been wounded. None of the wounds were very serious. Those who had them wound be able to ride. Four horses had been killed. The men who lost them wound take the horses of the men who had died. Their bodies were loaded onto the pack mules. Once the dead were loaded and the wounds were patched up, the Rangers stood around talking about what had happened.

Captain Jacob Long said, "Now that his cover is blown, he won't be coming back to Austin. But what do we do now? What chance do we have of ever catching him over here on this side of the river? He'll just stay where he's safe."

"You're forgetting one thing," replied Captain Jedidiah Trumbull. "Texas is his home. He just goes to Mexico to get away from us, but he don't love it over thar. He loves Texas and hates us for being here, and he hates all the settlers as well, who by the way, are on his land. He will always come back."

"I think you're right," said Captain Pete Blankenship. "We haven't been able to get our hands on him because he has always known what we were going to do. But now that has changed. We can come up with a way of gettin' him without him knowing about it in advance. Maybe."

Sullivan took in all that was said. He knew somebody needed to do something, but they were always hampered by their inability to follow the Indians across the river. Maybe somebody ought to just break the rules, try it and see if it worked.

The companies could not go into Mexico, but maybe one man could get away with it. If he suggested that Blankenship would say no, do not try that, period.

As the companies moved out headed for Austin, Sullivan slowed his horse, and said to those near him, "I need to tighten up my saddle. I'll catch up."

He stopped, got off his horse, hooked his left stirrup over his saddle horn, and watched the Rangers as they rode on.

47

Toombs Sullivan waited until the three Ranger companies were out of sight. Then he got back on his horse and turned his head toward the river. He slowly walked him in that direction. With each step his horse made across that one hundred yards he wondered if he was doing the right thing, the wrong thing, the crazy thing, the suicidal thing. Why was he going up against all those Indians by himself? The answer was simple. Because nobody else would do it. The Rangers would not go after them as a company or three companies, and no other individual would do it. So, it fell to him. He had to do it. Besides he was not going after all those Indians. He wanted just one of them. That made it even.

He got to the water's edge and stopped. He looked out across the river into the trees and growth along the other bank. He wondered if there was some lone Indian just waiting there for a white man. But no, that was not the case. He knew it.

He gently nudged his heels into the sides of his horse and said, "C'mon, Boy."

The horse stepped off into the water and they slowly went across. Sullivan held his rifle in his right hand just in case and also to keep it dry just in case his horse stepped in a hole.

When he reached the other side, he got down and walked for a short ways looking at the tracks of the Indian ponies in order to see which way they went. Much to his surprise the tracks turned up north along the river instead of going on west as he had thought they would.

So, what did that mean, he wondered. Were they staying near the river so they could make another raid into Texas very soon or were they going to cross again and go after the Ranger companies? Maybe it was a good thing he had come over to track them.

Sullivan followed the tracks for about a mile when suddenly he saw the Comanches had crossed the river again going back into Texas. He went back across knowing now that they were going to catch up to the Rangers and ambush them from behind or from the sides again.

When Sullivan reached the Texas bank, after crossing the river a second time, he rode hard to catch the Comanches. He could tell from their tracks that they were riding hard as well, anxious to catch the Rangers.

Soon he could see their dust, and became aware he was gaining on them. He went up a small rise and could not only see the Comanches ahead of him but also the Rangers ahead of them. Within minutes he was two hundred yards behind them and they were about three hundred yards behind the Rangers, who were taking their time.

He stopped his horse and put his rifle up to his right shoulder. He fired two quick shots, not so much to hit an Indian but to alert the Rangers. Three Indians turned around and came charging at him, while the rest of them began to fan out as they attacked the Rangers who had stopped and turned around.

Now both groups were firing at each other. Sullivan could see Indians falling off their horses, but his immediate concern was those coming at him. He got off his horse, never a wise thing to do he knew, having been told that several times, but it would enable him to make a better shot. He knelt down on one knee and dropped the Comanches, one after another.

He got back on his horse and charged at the Comanches. He was close to them now so he stopped again and began shooting at them, hitting a couple of them. Other Rangers were shooting them down. Rider-less Indian ponies were wandering around, running off in all directions.

The Rangers now charged at the Comanches, causing them to begin scattering, most of them riding quickly back toward the river. More of them were being hit and falling off their ponies. It did not appear that any of the Rangers were being hit at all.

Sullivan rode toward the river and the Indians crossing it. He kept firing at them, hitting a few of them. They seemed unaware now that he was shooting at them. Their main concern was the safety of Mexico.

Then Sullivan saw him, a tall figure on a white pony in the middle of the pack of Comanches. It was him, Nacona Pledger.

All of the Comanches were in the water now, some reaching the other side with their usual display of boasting and rifle waving. A few were shot off their ponies and were slowly drifting down the river.

When Sullivan reached the banks of the river he stopped and fired several more times. The Indians turned and began riding away. And Sullivan knew there was just one thing to do.

48

He heard Captain Blankenship calling his name, "Sullivan! Sullivan!" But he never even turned around or acknowledged that he heard him.

In no time he was out on the bank in Mexico again. He had noticed that the Indians had scattered once they crossed the river. They made no attempt to stay together. He had seen which way Nacona Pledger went by himself, which had always seemed to be what he did. He would not be hard to follow.

Sullivan cleared the area where there were trees, pulled out his binoculars and stood tall in his stirrups. He saw a trail of dust in the distance and a white pony in front of it. It had to be him. He was alone.

He would try to get as close to him as he could, and then when he stopped, he would possibly have a shot at him, maybe a long one, but at least a shot. He preferred doing this long distance rather than too up close and too personal. He just hoped he would not turn around and look and also that none of his braves would trail along after him.

His opportunity came quicker than he had imagined it would. He saw Nacona Pledger got down off his pony, and begin walking, giving his pony a rest, but never looking back.

Sullivan stopped, hopped down off his horse, knelt down as he had before, and took careful aim. Nacona was almost two hundred yards away. He knew he could hit him, but he might also miss him. He would take the chance. He held his breath and gently squeezed the trigger. He saw a little puff of dust fly up in the air just behind Nacona. He had missed him.

Now here he came after leaping up on his pony, firing his rifle as he drew closer and closer.

Sullivan could not get a clear shot at him. There was but one thing to do, shoot the horse, shoot the horse. He aimed at the horse just under his neck and fired. The pony tumbled forward with Nacona flying over his head and rolling on the ground. He picked up his rifle and started firing at Sullivan again.

Sullivan fired once, and then nothing but a click. He was out of ammo, having not reloaded since he first started shooting Indians, a serious mistake.

He saw Nacona throw down his rifle, being out of bullets also. Now at least they were even. Maybe.

Nacona came running at him firing his pistol wildly. Sullivan pulled out his pistol, took careful aim, and fired, hitting him. Nacona fell to the ground, got up and came running again. Sullivan fired again, hitting him a second time. Again, Nacona got up and was running toward him, firing his pistol. He then dropped it and pulled out a knife.

Suddenly he was on Sullivan, knocking him down. The pistol went one way and Sullivan the other. Sullivan jumped up as Nacona lunged at him. He grabbed Nacona's knife hand with both of his hands, but with his left hand Nacona pulled at Sullivan's head and flipped him over and down. As Nacona fell at him, Sullivan rolled out of the way. He scrambled to his feet ready to face him again. Nacona slashed at him with his knife, but Sullivan jumped back avoiding it. This happened three

206

times, but on the third time Sullivan threw himself at Nacona's legs tripping him. When Nacona started to get up Sullivan was already on his feet. He kicked Nacona in the face knocking him back. Nacona had lost the knife. He lunged at Sullivan, grabbed him and threw him over. Sullivan landed on his own pistol, felt it under his back. As Nacona dove at him he rolled over, took the pistol in his hand and shot Nacona in the chest as he started to get up. The impact of the bullet knocked him backward. He lay on his back, his dead eyes staring out at nothing, his lungs no longer breathing, his heart no longer beating, having been spilt open by the bullet.

Sullivan stood up. He quickly looked all around to make sure no other Indian had come upon them. He looked back at Nacona Pledger and thought, so this is the mystery ghost. Not so scary now. And you are no longer a mystery. You have been exposed and deposed. He's much bigger than I had thought, never thinking much about the size of Joe Joe Buffalo. No more trouble out of you. No more killing innocent people. You just lie here until you rot or the coyotes eat you or better still the buzzards and rats.

Sullivan reloaded his pistol and jammed it down under his belt. He picked up his rifle and reloaded it. He saw his horse a few yards away, and said, "C'mon, Boy, let's go to Texas."

He got back on his horse and headed toward the river.

49

As the day began to fade away Sullivan stopped to sleep for a while, maybe most of the night. He had the desire to just ride until he got to Austin, but it was a three-day trip, and he did not want to kill his horse. So, he stopped, took the saddle off his horse, and spread his blanket for the night.

It was good to stop and rest. It had been an exhausting day. The battle and the fight with Nacona Pledger had taken more out of him than he had imagined.

He propped his back against his upside-down saddle, and looked up at the stars. They were still there, still the same, never changing. There are some things, he thought, that just never . . . .

. . . . She came to him by the river. He had not seen her in a long time. She asked where he had been as the light wind made ripples in the tall grass near the trees and the limbs of the trees swayed and the leaves turned slightly. Her long hair gently fell around her right shoulder and moved a little with the breeze. She still had the same smile and the same blue eyes. Her gentle ways reached out to him and took him in as they always had. His heart was full and overflowing. He tried to speak to her, but when he reached for her she was gone. . . .

He was startled awake. He looked around and looked up at the stars again, and then he remembered where he was and what had happened. And he wondered where she had gone.

When he finally made it into Austin, he took his horse to the livery stable. He took off his saddle, parked it on a rack, took his saddle bags and rifle in his hands and walked over to the saloon. He put his gear down near the door against the wall. Then he stepped up to the bar and said, "Whiskey."

"Well, well, he has returned," said Lydia Langley as she walked up next to him. "I 'bout thought the Indians got you."

"Yeah, me too," he said as he turned up his glass.

"How did you survive out there? It's been a hot few days."

"Hot as the dickens, but that's the heat of Texas."

The End

CPSIA information can be obtained
at www.ICGtesting.com
Printed in the USA
LVHW050339261120
672644LV00013B/595